D1231574

WINTERKILL

WINTERKILL

by
GARY PAULSEN

THOMAS NELSON INC., PUBLISHERS

Nashville • New York

First edition

Library of Congress Cataloging in Publication Data

Paulsen, Gary.
  Winterkill.

  SUMMARY: An unhappy thirteen-year-old is befriended and protected by Duda, the tough cop of a small Minnesota town.
  [1. Police—Fiction] I. Title.
PZ7.P2843Wi   [Fic]   76-22807
ISBN 0-8407-6518-5

For Ralph Weinstock

WINTERKILL

Chapter One

I first met Duda in the spring.

It was 1954 and I had just turned thirteen and the fish were running in the spillway below the dam where it shoots out the bottom end of town—down below the railroad tracks and the big peeling sign that says: TWIN FORKS, MINNESOTA, WHERE SIX THOUSAND SMILING FACES GREET YOU TO THE FINEST FISHING IN THE WORLD! Which wasn't exactly true, really. They didn't all smile, and while sometimes you could nail some pretty fair walleyes, the fishing wasn't anywhere near being the finest in the world. Even I knew that. But I guess they had to plug the town someway or other, and fishing was about all they had—fishing and farming.

What really got me about the sign wasn't the words but the picture painted below them. There was a pretty woman waterskiing on a river in the background and in the forward part a guy was catching a fish that looked like a cross between a trout and an alligator. I mean I'd caught a lot of fish in Twin Forks, but nothing that ever looked like that.

Anyway, it was spring, like I said, and the fish were running—mostly suckers, but some walleyes, too, and now and then a big northern. There were about eight of us, I guess, or maybe ten, all kids except for old Carl Sunstrum, who was what you'd call the town drunk, or wino. Funny, none of the grownups in town liked Carl—they were always putting him down and all—but kids thought he was great, maybe because he was so much like us in a way. I mean he wasn't caught up in all that grown-up stuff about holding down a job or making a living. Come spring he'd be down at the dam with us, showing us how to wire sinkers underneath the snag hooks or how to put a good fisherman's knot in the line so we wouldn't lose it when we tied into a ten- or fifteen-pounder. He smelled pretty rough, especially his breath when he got down close to show you something, but we never minded because that was just part of old Carl, like the green wine bottle, or the tattered, beat-up sheepskin jacket he wore all the time. Somebody once told me he'd worn it when he flew a bomber during World War II, only I didn't believe it because he looked too old to have done that.

Thing is, nobody really knew anything about old Carl except that one day he showed up in town—some say he came in on a freight—and after that he was just always around, carrying a green bottle and not bothering anyone, hanging around the kids during the summer and the Mint Bar and Café during the winter, when it was too cold to be outside. I once asked him how he knew so much about fishing and he just smiled and said, "Because I know Jesus, and he knows fish," which didn't make any sense to me at all so I never asked him much again.

Whatever the reason, he really knew how to fish, that was certain. That day I met Duda, old Carl was working the worst part of the spillway, down below all the kids, so any fish he got along the concrete wall were ones we'd missed, and he still had over a hundred pounds of walleyes and maybe three hundred pounds of suckers. Which would buy a lot of wine. You could sell the suckers to the locker plant for twenty-five cents a pound—they resold them to mink farmers—or peddle the walleyes in the bars, and if you waited until people got drunk you'd sometimes get two bucks for a three-pounder.

I was just working my hook, a big, three-pronged job with double barbs on each prong, up along the cement wall, waiting for the bump—what you'd do is throw your hook in upstream and let it "walk" down

11

along the wall; when you felt it bump that meant it had hit a fish on the nose and you jerked up hard to set the barbs in him—when the kid next to me poked his elbow in my ribs and said, "Cop!" I looked up, across the spillway, which was about thirty feet wide, and there was Duda.

He was in uniform, standing with his hands tucked into his jacket pockets, and I'll have to admit at first he scared me a little. I mean he was so big and all black and shiny with leather harness and the shiny gun and silver badge and even black fur on the collar of his leather jacket. A cigarette was hanging tough out the corner of his mouth, and he had to tip his head sideways and put one ear in the fur on the collar of his jacket so the smoke wouldn't get into his eyes. I mean he really looked *tough*, and I'd had a few run-ins with cops because my folks drank and fought all the time. . . .

So we naturally scattered. But I'd only gone a few feet when I looked around and saw old Carl wasn't moving, and I thought what the hell am I running for, I haven't done anything really wrong, so I turned around and came back and stood next to Carl and waited.

For a minute nobody moved. It was like one of those phony scenes in movies where people just stand and stare at each other, like they mean something, only it never happens that way in real life. Except that this time it did seem to mean something; nothing real that I could pin down, but I stared across that water at him, and he stared at me, and it was like old Carl wasn't there anymore—like it had turned into some kind of dumb contest or something, to see who could stare the other guy down.

So in about a minute I looked down because snagging walleyes is wrong. You know how it is—you get to thinking like that when a cop looks at you, wondering what it is you must have done wrong, and snagging walleyes—not suckers, just walleyes—is wrong. The thing is it's not cop wrong, only game-warden wrong, and there's a lot of difference between the two in Twin Forks. Cops are for when you do something wrong that might hurt other people, like rob or drive drunk or something. Game wardens are for when you do something that doesn't bother other people much but is wrong in a different way—although I've never figured out why it's wrong to snag walleyes when you can take them with bait. But there you are; rules are rules.

Whichever way it is, snagging them is wrong, and when a cop gets to staring at you, no matter what kind of wrong it is, pretty soon you look down.

When I looked back up he was gone, and about a minute later he was on our side of the spillway—he'd had to walk back around the power plant—standing above us on the dirt bank.

"You." He pointed at me with his chin. "Get up here."

I looked at Carl but he was staring down into the water the way people do when they don't really want to look at anything but don't want to look too interested in what's going on around them, either, so

I shrugged and went up the bank and stood looking up at Duda.

"You trying to be wise or something?"

"What do you mean?" Up close like this I could see he had blue eyes and kind of a hooked nose and even though he kept his head tilted sideways that way, the smoke got into his right eye.

"I mean that bit across the spillway, you little puke. That's what I mean—that look you were giving me."

Thing is, his eyes weren't looking as tough as he was trying to sound. Still, I started to feel a little shaky inside. "I don't know what you mean. I mean I wasn't giving you a look or anything. . . ."

"Shut up." He said it bored. "I may be new around here, but I pick up on things fast. I find out you're a wise guy and you'll be wearing a collar around your neck—a bright-red one. It'll be your tongue tied around it, understand?"

I nodded and tried to look the way I figured he wanted me to look, but I was thinking that I'd heard somebody say they'd hired a new cop a week or two back because Twin Forks had grown and two weren't enough anymore. This must be the new one.

"What's in the sack?" He cut in on my thinking and pointed, again only with his chin and the cigarette, down by the spillway where I had my gunnysack.

"Fish."

"Any walleyes in that sack?"

I pushed one shoulder up and let it down. "Not

14

that I know of . . ." Which was of course a lie, but I wasn't going to tell him the truth. Not then. I mean he was *big*.

"Bring it up here and dump it."

"You mean the sack?"

"*Move.*"

So I brought the gunnysack up and turned it over and wouldn't you know a ten-pound walleye chock-full of eggs came out on top and lay there all glistening in the sun.

"Well." He touched the fish with the end of his boot—he was wearing those ankle-high flight boots and they were so spit-shined that I could see the walleye in the toe. "What's that?"

"What?" I could feel my face getting red.

"Don't be a puke head."

"I guess it's a walleye," I mumbled.

"Say again? Louder, boy."

"It's a walleye," I said louder.

"You got a pocketknife?"

Now what? I thought. Is he going to see if I've got weapons or something? I nodded.

"Clean the fish."

"You mean here?"

"You deaf, boy? Clean the fish before I club you."

So I took out my knife and cut her down the stomach and pulled out the eggs and air bladder and scraped out the blood pouch and wiped her out with the corner of the burlap sack. When I got done I stood up.

He looked downstream from the dam to where

15

there were some willows. "Go down there and cut a fork out of one of those willows. One that looks like a Y with one part of the Y twice as long as the other."

It took a minute or so but I found the right kind and cut it and brought it back, wondering what he was going to do.

"Now string the fish on the short part of the Y— through the gills—and hand it to me." He took one hand out of his pocket and held it out.

Actually it did make kind of a neat stringer, but I didn't let on I was surprised. I handed him the fish.

"And that, punk kid, is your introduction to graft." He held the walleye away from his pants and walked up toward the power plant, where I guess he'd parked the squad car. "Next time I see you down here I don't want to have to say anything. I just want to see a blur while you pick out the best wall-eye and clean it and get it on a stick for me. You understand?"

I nodded.

He stopped and looked past me to the fence again and his voice changed to a different tone—almost soft. "Oh, Carl, I almost forgot."

Old Carl turned and looked up at him. "Yeah, Nuts?"

"Bonnie said to come by—she's got some work for you or something."

"Sure, Nuts, I'll do that. And thanks."

"No sweat. Just carrying the word." And he left without even looking at me again.

I went back down to the fence and started swinging my hook next to Carl. Out of the corner of my eye I could see other kids starting to come back now that the cop was gone, and I didn't want the hole next to him filled. For a while we just fished. I got a couple of suckers and he got a nice walleye, and then the run seemed to die off a little—it came and went—so I rolled in my line and just watched Carl work his hook.

"You know him, huh?"

He looked at me out of the corner of his eye. "People like me always know the police. It's natural, like rain."

"No, I mean from before somewhere."

He shook his head. "Just met him last week. But I know his type—good cop."

"*Tough,* you mean."

Carl's arms moved with the hook. "Depends. Not always so tough—just depends."

"You called him Nuts. Is that his name?"

"Naww—nickname. His real name is Duda. Something Duda—I don't know his first name. They call him Nuts because . . ." He looked at me, sizing me up. "Well, just because." He pulled the green bottle out of his flight-jacket pocket and took a long swallow. "Was I you, the next time he comes down on you I'd just call him sir."

"Yeah, I guess you're right. What was that other stuff—about Bonnie or somebody?"

But Carl didn't answer—I guess because it was none of my business, which it wasn't. For the rest of the day we fished, and when it started to get dark I

17

hauled my sack up to the bars and sold what I'd caught for almost thirty dollars, which was five dollars more than I needed to buy Art Overbye's 1934 Dodge.

Chapter Two

I bought the Dodge the next morning, and even though it didn't run—it had a cracked block—that didn't matter much because I couldn't drive anyway. All that mattered was that I had a car. It took us almost four hours, but we finally got it pushed from Art's place over to the driveway of the crummy apartment building where I lived. Old man Klein, the landlord, had said I could park it there as long as I wanted if I hauled clinkers during the winter from the furnace up to where the trash truck could get them.

That first night I slept in the back seat, just getting the feel of her, you know, and that was all right; just feeling the soft coarseness of the upholstery on my cheek and reading by the light of the little lamp in the ceiling, which barely glowed on the old battery. As far as looks went she was all right—nothing wrong except for a small tear in the front seat and a dent in the left door. The way I had it figured, by the time I learned to drive I'd probably have enough saved up from fishing and whatnot to buy a block from Phillips' junkyard, and Art, who was taking auto mechanics in vocational school and knew about cars, could help me put it in, and wham! I'd have me a car.

Just goes to show how you shouldn't make all those plans, because it wasn't two days after I got the car that Mom and Dad got drunk and had one of their fights—this one a little wilder than most—and I walked in right in the middle of it. So right away whatever it was they'd been fighting about was *my* fault, as it usually was when they were drunk, which they were most of the time, and the next thing I knew I was back under the kitchen table and Mom was screaming and trying to jab me with a butcher knife.

She got me only once, and then just a little cut in the leg—it hardly bled at all—and I tried to tell the judge, later at the hearing the social worker made us go to, that I didn't mind the conditions I lived with, that for the most part it was pretty good around the house. But he didn't listen and I got foster-homed for the summer.

The judge called it a probationary foster homing or something like that, the idea being that at the end of the summer I could come home and we'd see how it worked out. But I think it was, as Duda told me later, my first real experience, not counting the walleye, with graft and corruption, because *I* didn't have anything to say about where I went. I mean I had relatives all over northern Minnesota on farms, neat uncles and cousins, where I sometimes spent summers anyway when I was just a kid, but do you suppose that judge would send me to one of them?

Instead he let a guy named Gib Nymen have me. It for sure soured me on religion, at the very least, and might just have ruined my life, although it's too soon to tell for certain.

Gib had a place ten miles east of Twin Forks, a two-hundred-acre dairy farm, and no kids of his own except for a new baby that didn't do anything all the time I was there but cry and puke. On top of that he had a weird wife. Gib would never read anything but the Bible or listen to anything but church music, and he liked to use his belt or part of a harness to beat kids. . . .

What I think is that he and the judge were old friends or something and had this agreement that the next kid who came through court and was old enough to work would go to Gib Nymen. That's what I think, just for the record.

Still, at first there for a while it wasn't so bad, before Gib decided I was a sinner and needed help. For a week or two it was almost nice. He took me out to the farm that first night and asked me how my leg felt and set me up in an upstairs room in the back part of the house all to myself and for the first day or so didn't make me do anything.

So I had no idea of what I was getting into until the third day. I more or less just wandered around the place, looking at things, helping out a little now and then and limping whenever his wife was around. Strange thing about that. I mean my leg didn't hurt at all, but every time Gib's wife came into view I'd start limping. Couldn't help it.

If I expected her to feel sorry for me I was wrong —she was just as mean as Gib. I think I did it because she stared at me all the time. It was downright weird, but whenever I came in range she'd start *staring* at me. Not like some people do, where if you look at them they look away, but all the time—even if I looked right at her she'd keep right on staring with these kind of washed-out gray eyes as though I wasn't really there. . . . It gave me the willies, and after a while I'd just get out of the way when she came around; get busy doing something.

On the third day—or actually night, because it wasn't day yet but dark as the inside of a cow—I finally got a smell of what the rest of the summer was going to be like, only I didn't catch it all for a couple of weeks. About four in the morning Gib tossed me out of the sack.

"All right—time to get up." He didn't wait for me but went out of the room and downstairs. I just rolled over and went back to sleep. I'd been having this really neat dream about Gale Storm and I was just getting to the point where it was interesting, if you know what I mean, when Gib came back upstairs.

"Get *up!*" he said, loud, and this time he jerked the covers until I fell out on the floor.

When I got downstairs Gib and his wife were sitting at the table, with the baby in the high chair crying. Gib had the Bible out and motioned with his hand for me to take a seat. In front of me when I sat down was a bowl of mush with a lump of bacon grease in the middle and a spoon stuck in the edge. Since there was nothing else on the table I grabbed the spoon and tucked in—even gunky mush was better than nothing.

Whap! He hit me under the table with his hand so hard that my knees knocked together. "We do *not* eat until we've heard the Lord's Word in this house."

And darned if he didn't read for *forty-five minutes,* while the mush got cold and the bacon grease turned to something that looked like wax and his wife stared a hole through my head and the baby just kept crying until she'd jam a spoonful of mush into its mouth, which would make it puke until it got all the mush out and then it'd cry again. . . .

All in all it was one of the worst breakfasts I've ever had; worse, even, than the later ones because then I knew what to expect. I mean that mush stuck to the roof of my mouth along with the grease for the better part of the day.

Once we got out in the barn and turned the lights on it was all right—at least those first few days. Gib sent me out to the pasture to get the cows. It was nice walking through the wet grass while the sun was coming up, and the cows took their time. Everything was coming down green—that's how they said it in Twin Forks when spring really got its teeth in and you knew summer wasn't far off. That first morning was kind of like a movie I'd seen once about Ireland—everything was so green and misty it almost looked like a movie set. Walking behind the cows, I started to daydream—you know how you do when your brain doesn't have to work on what you're doing. I imagined I was in a faraway land somewhere, where nobody was allowed to live in the country unless he was under fourteen or fifteen, and the only rule was that everybody had to do what they did best and enjoyed doing. . . .

I guess I'll have to admit it was kind of a hokey dream, but that doesn't change the fact that I had it or how I felt that morning—like if that morning could have just gone on and on forever somehow, with me just walking in back of those Holsteins until the end of time, I probably wouldn't have minded much.

But before long we got to the barn and the argument between Sue and Emily (I learned their names later) started and I forgot all about the daydream, at least for a while. Sue and Emily were something I've never been able to figure out unless maybe it's

24

just that cows are a lot more like people than they're supposed to be.

I mean Gib had thirty-one cows that he milked every morning and every night. And every morning and every night they'd come in from the pasture, except in the winter, when they stayed in all the time. They'd go to their stalls in the barn and put their heads through the stanchions and never get mixed up and just stand there, waiting for you to come along and close the stanchions around their necks and milk them.

Except for Sue and Emily. They fought. Every single morning and every single night they'd start in the door and Sue would head down to the far end of the barn where Emily's stall was, and Emily would tear around trying to get in front of her and butt her out of the way back down to her own stall. If that didn't work she'd go and stand in Sue's stall and bellow like somebody was kicking her in the stomach until you pushed and pulled and got them in the right stalls. Darnedest thing I've even seen. That first morning I got caught in the middle of them and got a little wind knocked out of me when Gib started heaving them back to their own stalls, so I got mad and when I got my breath back I went into the compressor room where Gib was putting the milking machines together.

"Why don't you just leave them where they want to go?" I asked.

"They wouldn't give any milk." He slid the rubber teat-cups into the metal holders. "It's God's way of showing that nothing comes without a little work."

That pretty much ended the conversation. I mean what can you say when a guy gives you an answer like that? I think maybe that's what got me down the most that summer, even more than some of the rougher stuff I'll talk about in a bit. No matter what happened, good or bad, it was always God's way of showing something as far as Gib was concerned. Like when I stepped on the silage fork and the handle came up and caught me in the stomach so hard I had to go in back of the barn and puke for a while. You think it was just because I didn't watch where I was walking? Not on your life. It was God's way of showing me that it's best to hang silage forks up when you're done using them, according to Gib.

Of course I can't speak for Gib—wouldn't want to if I could—but as far as I'm concerned, if God thinks he has to slam me with a fork handle just to get my attention, I'm not sure I want to have anything to do with Him.

But to get back to Sue and Emily. It was their fault, really, that I turned into a sinner, which led to my trying to kill Gib with a manure fork and my running into Duda again the hard way, like he used to say.

But that was all at the end of the summer.

Chapter Three

I learned a lot about farming that summer, so I guess
it wasn't all wasted. Say what you like about Gib,
and I said a lot about him that I wouldn't put in a
book, he could farm better than most. I've never
seen fatter cows or better-tended fields—no mustard
at all on any of his land, which was something, considering that all the farms around were almost solid
yellow with the stuff.

But he did it wrong, somehow. I mean farming
really boils down to an awful lot of hard work. I

knew that from visiting my cousins. When I'd want to play there was always something they had to do, like feed the chickens or sweep the granary out or open this gate or close that other one—never a minute to get out there and play except on Sundays. But there's two kinds of hard work. There's the kind that makes you ache all over so you hope you *never* see another pitchwork, like when you're getting hay in and it looks like rain; but while you feel pain when you go to bed, there's also a nice feeling—like maybe there was a contest and you won something. The other kind of hard work is when you bust your tail all day but when you go to bed you feel like you *didn't* win the contest, like maybe it was all wasted somehow. Later I tried once to explain it to Duda and he said he understood but couldn't make it clear to people, either, except that it had something to do with smiling or not smiling just before you went to sleep, which didn't make any sense to me then.

Take that mustard. Other farmers would let it grow until their fields were so yellow that you couldn't tell what the crop was supposed to be. Then a farmer would load a spray tank on his back and walk around the field and spray the mustard dead. Do that twice in a summer and that's all you had to mess with it—done and done, like they say in Twin Forks.

Gib went out and *picked* it—every night, unless it was raining. After chores and working all day long we'd eat, and when other people were sitting on their porches listening to the robins and frogs, Gib would collar me and drag me out to the fields and we'd pick mustard by hand until ten or ten thirty, pulling the plants out by the roots and throwing them in back of us. It was all kind of eerie. I mean the first night or two we did it I worked next to him and it scared me a little. He was big and had these shoulders that sloped down to his arms too much, and he'd bend only a little to get the plant and he'd tear it out like it was something alive that he wanted to kill. Once I heard him mumbling under his breath but couldn't make out the words, and after that I'd move off in the darkness and lay back between the rows and watch the stars while Gib worked around ripping out the plants. He didn't seem to notice that I wasn't tearing out weeds—like he noticed if I didn't do some other things—and it gave me time to think now and then.

Which wasn't too good, because out there in the dark, when it was all warm and summery about the first thing that came to mind was Gale Storm or somebody like her—a couple of times Jane Russell from a movie I'd seen that she was in—and that would lead to what Gib called bad thoughts, which led to sinning, you know. . . .

It seemed like I sinned a lot that summer—more than Gib knew about, that's for sure. I mean I had some thoughts so downright bad I could hardly think straight.

But what I was getting to was the hard-work part. After a night of picking mustard on top of a day of working in the fields you got awfully tired, so it was like somebody had poured sand inside your eyes, and when you finally hit the pillow you were out before you could think.

But, like Duda said, you didn't have that smile just before, and so in the morning you didn't want to get up and do it again.

It was the wrong kind of hard work. And so it was just natural that I'd start taking my feelings out on whatever I happened to be doing.

Like bringing Emily and Sue in for milking. I'd been going on pushing them around for a week or two, I guess, when it suddenly got to me that I was letting a couple of cows get the best of me. So one morning when I was getting them in I rushed into the barn ahead of the cows and grabbed a pitch-fork, and when Emily and Sue started their game I started jabbing them a little.

Next thing I knew I was up in the air and Gib had me by the collar and was hitting me on the hind end so hard my teeth almost turned to powder.

"Don't ever do that!" he was screaming. "It's a *sin*, it's a *sin*, it's a *sin*. . . ." And he'd nail me hard each time he said *sin*. At first I tried to get loose but couldn't, so I just hung there and let him hit me, figuring out ways I could kill him later—you know the way you do.

When he put me down I took off and didn't come back for the rest of the day—just hung around in the back pasture, sulking.

Then I started thinking how it was probably wrong for me to stick the cows with a fork in the first place

30

and how Gib probably didn't realize how hard he'd hit me—I was all black and blue—so I ambled back to the house about suppertime.

It was like nothing had happened. I sidled back into the house and there was a plate of food and Gib had the Bible out, so we listened to him read and we ate and I went up to bed and I thought that was the end of it.

Three or four days later, I forget exactly, we started haying and I'd forgotten all about the beating —although I noticed Gib looking at me funny now and then—when I accidentally slammed Emily's stanchion too tight and she bellowed before I could get it loose. Before I could think, I was up in the air and Gib was working me over again, this time with a piece of harness or a belt, it was hard to tell, hanging like that. But he was really screaming: "SIN, SIN, SIN," while he whipped me and his voice kept rising higher and higher and his breathing was funny. "Got to whip the *sin* out!" he finally screamed and I broke loose and headed for the back pasture again.

I mean it was like he was laying for me to do something wrong that time, and I hadn't really meant to do anything anyway. Really scary.

That time I bled some, not much, but it hurt when I went to the can and I was awful careful when I went back into the house later.

Again it was like nothing had happened. Food on the table, the whole shot—just like normal. I ate and went up to bed and thought it out. I mean your normal kid would probably have shagged about then, but I'd been raised different, what with my folks and their drinking and all. So I just figured it was something wrong with Gib, the way the booze was with my folks, and I'd just have to be more careful around him or he'd send me back to the judge and I'd wind up in a reform school or something.

I thought for quite a while, and I guess I cried some and called Gib a few names that he'd have beat the devil out of me for if he'd heard them and finally I went to sleep feeling kind of lonesome.

After haying was done it was time for the harvest and in only another month it would be back to school. Things were going pretty well, what with me doing most of the milking and barn work alone while Gib went out to the fields. I was getting good with the cows—even had Emily and Sue figured out to where I'd just let them sort it out while I got the milkers ready to use. It only took them a minute and they'd go to their own stalls without shoving or anything. And Gib was wrong. They gave as much milk as always, and I thought about telling Gib one morning at breakfast—mush with bacon grease as usual—but decided it might be pushing my luck. He didn't come out to the barn at all anymore, which suited me just fine, and I couldn't see any profit in goading him.

Actually what happened was that I got *too* good at milking. I had a system going toward the end there, and it took me only an hour and a half in the morning and two hours at night, longer in the evening because I swabbed out and disinfected the gutters and all. (I mean old Gib had a grade-A dairy—everything white and stainless steel and *clean*. You could eat out of the gutters.)

Well, wouldn't you know Gib saw I had some spare time going when he caught me trying to shoot some barn swallows under the barn eaves with a bow and arrow I'd made from a Juneberry bush, and the next thing I knew he had me on a tractor spreading manure. Not that I minded driving the tractor; that part was fun. But I had to load the manure with a fork from the pile in back of the barn, and that was hard work and not particularly nice because some of his calves and chickens had died and he'd just thrown them in the manure pile and they were what Duda would have called ripe.

The thing is if the truth were known I didn't know that much about tractors, and Gib didn't tell me much except how to steer and shift. So one morning I was hooking up the spreader and I only had about an inch to move it backward. I'd heard about this trick where you leave the key in the ignition on off and put the tractor in reverse and hit the starter a little and it was supposed to jerk back just a hair. So I decided to try it.

The problem was Gib's tractor was a Case 40-D, the D on the end meaning diesel, and I didn't know that with a diesel even if the key is off it can start and run if it's warm.

Well, wouldn't you know the dumb thing started and backed completely over the manure spreader—

just sort of walked right up the hitch, crunching and screeching and chewing all the way back across the bed and down on the ground again and was half-way to the barn before I could get unscrambled from where I'd landed when I'd jumped to get out of the way. I caught her there and got her in neutral, but the damage was done.

Not to the tractor. Those Case 40-D jobbers are tough. But the spreader wasn't meant to carry tractors, and it pretty much flattened the thing so it'd never spread manure again, and I figured I might as well just get out of the county right then. I mean if Gib nailed me the way he did for just making his cow cut up a little, think what he'd do to me for crushing his old spreader.

I didn't get halfway across the yard, and I was walking pretty fast, too, when I saw him coming. He'd been in the field just east of the granary, close to the house, and seen the whole thing, so I changed plans—he was coming like a bull I'd once seen at Uncle Harvey's place who charged a dog that had been messing with him—and headed for the barn. I'm not sure why I didn't keeping running except that something in me said to make it to the barn— maybe because I'd spent so much time in there that it was like home or something.

Whatever the reason, it was a mistake. I ran in the front door and halfway down between the gutters before I realized the back door was locked from the outside, and when I turned around to whip back out the front, it was too late.

Gib was there. And just looking at him scared me so much I almost wet my pants. He was hunched over a little and breathing funny like—either from running or just crazy—and I'll be a liar for the rest of my life if he wasn't *smiling*. Not a nice smile—the way a skull smiles when the really hairy part of the movie hits you and you slouch down in your seat. And still smiling he reached out sideways and unhooked a trace chain that was hanging on the wall and kind of swung it so the chain part rattled when it hit the cement floor. Man, I thought, if he catches me with that end it'll tear my head off.

So there wasn't anywhere to run, he had me cornered cold, and the only thing I could find was that old manure fork leaning by the door to the separator room, and I grabbed it and went right for his guts with it. Way I saw it, there was no sense messing around; if I didn't kill him, he was sure to kill me.

I suppose if he hadn't deflected the fork at the last second with the chain, I probably *would* have killed him, too, but he knocked it down and two of the tines on the side went into his leg as easy as pushing a spoon in mush. I remember being surprised as all get out when they went in so easy.

Which was about the last thing I remember because Gib threw away the trace, pulled the fork out of his leg like he was swatting a fly, picked me up and threw me into the separator room so hard that everything tumbled over and over and I couldn't think at all for a while.

I don't know how long I was out like that, maybe an hour while I couldn't really tell what was going on. Now and then I could feel things—I guess Gib was working me over some more, because later I was all covered with cuts and lumps. At the time I didn't feel much of it or really know what was happening —just thumps and scrapes from being rubbed on the cement floor. And I guess when he got sick of beating on me he called the cops.

Because when I could finally see things at least a little clear, the first thing I focused on were those shiny flight boots, and when I looked up Duda was standing in the doorway of the separator room. He had that cigarette in his mouth and his head tilted sideways, and he was looking half on the edge of smiling.

"The wiseacre kid from the dam." It wasn't a question—more like he was talking about how it might rain. "Figured I'd be running into you again. Wiseacre kids always show up again. Anything broke?" He gestured at me, so I looked down and I could see why he asked—I was ripped up so you couldn't tell if I was wearing clothes or rags.

I moved a little and nothing crunched, so nothing was broken, but I hurt so bad I started crying, which made me madder than hell because for some reason when Duda was around you didn't want to cry. "No —I'll be all right." I tried to get up but that didn't work so well, so I settled for kind of half crouching by the separator stand.

"Care to give me your side of it?" He shrugged

like it didn't matter. "Or do you want to wait until you see the judge?"

"Judge? Why should we see a judge?"

"For the hearing. It's what you normally do when you're charged with assault with a deadly weapon, attempted murder and all. . . ."

"For sticking somebody with a manure fork when they're trying to kill *you*?" I yelled.

"Yelling won't help."

"Well."

Nobody said anything for a long time. I sat there wondering what Gib had said when he called the police and Duda just stood watching me, waiting. I guess finally he got sick of listening to me sniffle.

"Talk. It won't hurt and might help." He squatted then, but careful so his uniform wouldn't get dirty.

So I told him the whole thing. I mean I didn't want to at first because I didn't want to sound like a crybaby, but you know how it is. I started talking and pretty soon I was crying and yakking away and the next thing I was telling him about the trouble with my folks, for crying out loud, and *everything* way back to when I was just a kid.

And he just sat there, listening, smoking and nodding once in a while. Never said a word until I was talked out, then he just stood up, straightened his pants and jacket and jerked his chin.

"Get out in the prowl car. I'll be with you in a minute."

"What are you going to do?"

"Move!"

So I went to the car and waited while he went into the house. He wasn't in there long—I'd only just started to lean back—when he came out, got in the car, and started out the driveway.

"Where are we going?" I've never been one to be able to stay quiet. Don't know why, just always been that way—when it gets quiet I have to talk.

"To a friend of mine. A farm." He chopped the words like he was mad at something.

"What for?"

"To put you to work—for money." A cigarette appeared in his hand and he lighted it. "Of all the sick pukes . . ." It was more a whisper than out loud.

"Who, Gib?" I couldn't really make out what he was talking about.

"Never mind. Look, kid, if you're lucky, really lucky, you might grow up—though looking at you it's hard to believe." He smiled, a tight little flash of teeth around the cigarette. "If you do make it, try to remember . . . ahh, the devil with it. Just grow up. That's all you have to remember."

"You mean somebody like Gib? Remember it when I grow up?"

"It's nothing. Never mind. Mr. Nymen dropped the charges and I'll talk to the judge and tell him you're at a different place. Now shut up and quit asking so many questions—you talk *all* the time."

It was something I'd get to see a lot of later. He'd open up and get what I'd call almost loose or soft and talk, and then he'd clam up and get almost mean. Like he hadn't meant to open up in the first place or was ashamed of it or something.

It threw me off at first, but I got used to it when I got to know him better. Like take his coming out to Gib's in the first place. It didn't make sense if you didn't know how Duda did things.

I mean we'd gone three or four miles without talking, with once in a while a staticky sound coming out of the radio, when I realized that Duda was a *town* cop. He had no business coming out to a farm like he did—that should have been a job for the sheriff, old Agil Peterson, not Duda, seeing as how it was outside the city limits a good ten miles.

But then that was before I learned how Duda worked things. . . .

Chapter Four

We didn't go back into Twin Forks at all. Duda took me straight to Gust Homme's place, which was a run-down little farm covered with kids. Or I should say it *seemed* to be run down and *seemed* to be covered with kids. When you got to looking around, there were only three kids, all little—I guess the oldest one was about four—and only the things that didn't matter looked run down. Like the barn, one of those old-fashioned ones with a kind of round roof—it could have used a coat or two of paint. But when

41

you started looking closer you could tell that the things that were important—like tractors or the stalls for the cows or the fence—were all in topnotch shape.

We pulled up in the yard and it was wild; dogs were barking, chickens scattering one way, geese the other, and kids came running out from under things to see who it was—all movement and sound, the two things I hadn't seen much of at Gib's.

Duda got out but I was ashamed of my clothes, so I stayed in the car while a kind of happy-looking fat guy with gray hair and bright-blue eyes came out to greet him, and then the two of them came over to my side of the car.

"Got one for you, Gust." That's how Duda put it. "Used to be over at Trontvet's. . . ." He let it hang there.

Gust looked in the window and shoved his hand through and shook mine, just like if I was a man, which made me feel good. "Welcome—we can always use another hand. What do you get?"

"Five a day and slops," Duda cut in. "I guarantee him for good work—don't I, runt?"

I nodded but didn't say anything. I mean it was all like a game they were playing—Gust's eyes were laughing—so I just played along.

"He's going to need some clothes, Gust." Duda made a small sign and the two of them went to the front of the car so I couldn't hear. Twice I made out the word "Nymen" and once I could see Gust's mouth move and I could have sworn he said something rough, but I couldn't be sure. When they

42

got done, Duda signaled me out of the car and we all walked toward the house with the kids following.

Just before we got to the door, it opened and the fattest woman I've ever seen stood there with her hands on her hips. "My goodness, Nuts, what have you got there?"

Duda laughed. "Just a puke kid, Alice. Couldn't keep out of trouble, so I brought him here—figured you could straighten him out if anybody could."

"That's not quite true, Mrs. Homme," I started, and I was going to tell her some of the truth, but I never got another word out. Have you ever had somebody wrap a big, soft, warm quilt around you when you're cold and it made you all cozy and warm? Well, that's about what happened. Alice Homme kind of wrapped around me and took me in the house, and before I knew it I was eating pie with cold milk and she had a pan of water and soap and a rag and was washing the cuts on my face and back, and even though I was thirteen I didn't mind.

I didn't even hear Duda leave—that's how nice it felt after being at Gib's place. And when I was pretty much patched up and had a gut full of pie, Gust came in and got me and showed me around the place.

He had twenty-five cows and eight pigs and some chickens and, like I said, geese. And it was all kind of messed together in a nice way. I mean the cows were out in the pasture, but the geese and chickens followed us around and the kids just ran back and forth playing and the dogs kept running up and

43

sticking their noses in our hands, and any question I asked, no matter how dumb it was, Gust would answer straight and like to a grown-up. Took me a while, but I finally worked up the courage and asked.

"When you and Duda were talking back there and you asked me how much and Duda cut in with five a day and slops—was that straight?"

Gust was checking the sickle teeth on the combine and he looked up and smiled. "Yup. If you work. Five dollars a day and all you can eat and a place to sleep. Why?"

"Oh, I was just wondering." Lord, I thought, why didn't that judge send me *here?* Another month till school and I'll be rich. Five dollars a *day.*

"That wasn't too good, over there at Nymen's, I guess?" Gust slid the sickle bar back into the guides.

"No." I couldn't think of anything else to say other than that, and that was the last time as long as I was around Gust that I ever heard anything about my having been over at Gib's.

"Well, guess we ought to get to work." He pulled out a tobacco can and offered me some but I turned it down. I'd tried tobacco once with my cousin Harlan and I've never *been* so green. "Can you milk?"

I nodded. "With machines."

"Good. Way we'll work her is the kids'll help you take care of chores around the house and I'll head out to the fields—got some barley and oats to get in. See you tonight."

And he jumped on the tractor with the combine

44

hooked to it and took off, leaving me standing and wondering what the blazes he meant about having the kids help me when, like I said, the oldest one was only four or so.

I didn't have long to wonder. He wasn't halfway down the driveway when I heard a bloodcurdling bellow come from the direction of the pigpen. When I ran over there I saw the middle kid—I can't for the life of me remember their names—was caught in the fence and the boar was looking like he might take a taste of her foot. It scared me cold. I'd never seen it but heard stories about mothers coming out to the pigpen to find just bits and pieces of their kids left from when the pigs ate them.

Well, I got that kid loose and about two minutes later I looked over and the oldest kid was trying to start the grain auger—a big screw in a tube thing for unloading grain from a truck or wagon into the granary—and almost had the motor on it cranked up, too, before I got him, or maybe it was a her, away from it. Lucky, too, because those augers will take a foot so fast you won't even know it's gone.

I'd no more than turned around when I happened to look in back of the barn and the youngest kid, only just able to walk, was crawling around under the bull out there—biggest Holstein I've ever seen—and though he didn't seem to mind much, you never know what bulls will do. So I snaked out there and got the kid from under and back in the main yard. I was just in time for number-two kid to come by with a goose egg and the maddest goose in the world screaming after him—or her—and while I was wrestling the goose down, which hurt some, I looked up and there was the oldest kid getting ready to jump off the *roof* of the granary. . . .

Uncle Harvey told me once about an old banty hen he had that couldn't have chicks of her own for some reason. One summer he was mowing June grass and killed a grouse with the mower because she wouldn't get off the nest. So he brought the eggs home for the banty to sit on and she hatched them out. Guess it made quite a sight, that hen leading those eight baby partridge around the yard. But grouse grow a lot faster than chickens, and learn to fly pretty quick, too, and before the summer was out I guess that old banty just about went nuts trying to keep those partridge chicks in line. She'd get them all herded into one place and set out to parade them across the barnyard the way banties do and two steps later one of them would be flying this way and another that way. Way Harvey told it, the hen just up and died of frustration. But Harvey has a way of making stories come out with the right ending even if it didn't really happen that way, so I don't known about that part.

But that's how I felt that first day at Gust's. I mean have *you* ever tried to milk twenty-five cows and want to do a really bang-up job because you're getting five bucks a day for it, and have three kids helping you by pulling the milkers off the cows as fast as you get them on? Talk about dying of frustration! When I looked up and saw the middle one chewing on one of those Holsteins, getting his *own* milk, I almost croaked. Twice I was about to go in and get Alice to mind the kids, but then I started thinking that if Gust had wanted it that way he would have told me, so I didn't.

Well, I somehow got the cows all milked, and the milk in cans, and the cans in the milk house and everything cleaned up and put away. But it was a trial, let me tell you, and when Gust rolled into the yard that night, with the grain wagon full of barley, which we augured into the granary, I was pretty well shot, so we didn't talk much until we went in to eat.

That's when I found out why Alice hardly ever left the house—she just stayed inside and *cooked* all day. Man, what a meal she put out! There was home-made bread and hot biscuits and boiled potatoes with butter and the kind of gravy you *like* to let slop all over your plate. And meat—Gust told me later it was canned moose meat from hunting the year be-fore—in a big bowl, all kind of stewed together with carrots and I think turnips or maybe rutabagas.

I mean we ate until I thought seams were going to pop all over me. And then when I thought we were done and I'd wrapped the last of my stomach around a tall glass of fresh, cold milk, darned if she didn't come out with not one but *two* pies and put them down on the table with a big pitcher of fresh cream so thick it didn't pour but kind of glopped out. . . .

It was all kind of like a dream. One of those pies was fresh crab apple and the other one was rhubarb, and I put a piece of each on my plate the way Gust did and took turns taking bites—first the crab apple, which was kind of sweet, then a shot of rhurbarb with that tang that made your tongue almost sit up for another bite of the apple.

I don't know how long I'll live, but if I get lucky and make a hundred, I bet I won't forget that meal.

And what really got me was the kids. None of them, not even the smallest one, cried or puked once through the whole thing—they just sat there like us and shoveled it in, and when we got done that table looked like an army had gone over it. Nothing was left.

"That was awfully good," was all I could say.

"Oh, I don't know." Gust was busy rolling a cigarette—he never chewed tobacco in the house. "In the main it wasn't bad, but I think there was one biscuit, back there toward the start, that might have been a touch heavy. . . ."

"Well, I *never!*" Alice was up and cleaning off the table. "Isn't that the berries, though? You cook and slave and what do you get? 'One biscuit was a touch heavy. . . .'"

But I could see they were both smiling and happy, so it was all right, it was something they did a lot, I found later—kind of kid each other privately even when other people were around.

"Have any trouble milking?" Gust turned to me. "Like with your help, maybe?"

"No—well, maybe it slowed me down." I thought

48

of the kid in the pigpen, another on the auger, or chasing the goose. "A little."

"Generally I try to keep them corralled in the cool house when I'm doing chores, but if that doesn't work I turn them loose on Jane—that swaybacked old lady down at the end on the north side. She can't have calves anymore and likes the attention. . . ."

"Oh. You mean you *let* them suck on that cow."

He nodded. "Why not? Saves washing a glass, is how I look at it. Besides, what with Alice in here all day whumping up them heavy biscuits" —he smiled — "you about go out of your mind trying to keep the kids out of everything."

I didn't say anything but I was thinking amen to that, and figuring I wasn't going to pay as much attention as I had this first day.

After a while it started to get evening outside and we moved out on the porch and Gust got a krokono board out and we sat and played for a while. Krokono is a game sort of like pool except you snap these doughnut wood things with your fingers and try to get them in little netted pockets. Gust was so good at it that I hardly got a shot, but that didn't matter because I was thinking of something else anyway.

Most of it was pretty silly because it was all about love and a bunch of other junk. Like I was trying to think if I loved Gust and Alice like a mother and father, or just liked them for being nice people, or what. And then Duda's picture came up and I started thinking about him, wondering how it was he knew Gust and why he came out to Gib's and got me. And then it hit me that it was only that morning that Gib and I had fought and it seemed like years. The next thing I knew my head just slumped down like it was made of lead and I didn't even feel it when Gust picked me up and carried me to the back bedroom. . . .

Chapter Five

Funny, but now, even though it's only been a year, I look back on that month at Gust's and I can't really remember it all the way it happened, day by day. Even now that I want to, because it was the only really nice time I ever had.

It comes through in kind of pictures, like scenes from a movie or something—some good and some not so good, maybe, but nothing bad. Sometimes when the dreams get bad and I wake up, I think about that time at Gust's place and the pictures come through and it makes it easier to get back to sleep. . . .

Like one day it was really hot and we'd been shoveling and augering oats all day, so we were covered all over and itching with chaff.

"The devil with it!" Gust said, throwing down the shovel he'd been using. "Let's go swimming!"

"Where can we go swimming?" I reached down and shook my pants—that's where chaff really gets you.

"Get on the drawbar; I'll show you."

So we unhooked the grain wagon and I stood on the drawbar of the tractor and he took her out and down the road about a mile where a small stream went under the road and made a pool. And we shucked down and jumped in.

"Can you dive?" Gust asked me, looking for all the world like a big old white whale except for his face and hands, which were burned red.

"Not without a diving board." I was scrubbing the chaff out of my armpits.

"Ha! I'm going to call your bluff."

He went back up to the tractor without dressing —which was brave considering we were right on the main road—and backed her down to the edge of the pool. Then he stood up on the seat, which was mounted on a big piece of spring-iron, and after two bounces did about half a somersault into the pool. He darn near emptied it.

I can close my eyes now and still see Gust standing up on that tractor seat, white as a fish belly, laughing and springing and kind of blubbering all over with fat.

And I remember one Sunday when Duda came out to see how I was doing. Or at least that's why I think he came out, though with Duda you could never be sure about anything.

Anyway, he brought a bottle and he and Gust just sat on the porch all day sipping from the bottle and drinking water now and then until they got drunk as lords, but in a nice way. Like they never got loud or fought or anything. Just sat there drinking quietly on the edge of the porch, and I sat down on the grass stripping dandelion stems with my thumbnail, listening—although, to be truthful, sometimes there wasn't much to listen to, the way they talked.

"You fought in that Korea business, didn't you, Nuts?" And Gust would take a sip and hand the bottle to Duda.

"Wouldn't call it fighting. Spent a lot of time digging, though. I guess I know more about Korean dirt than most folks."

"Ha!" Gust would say, and slap his leg and take another sip. "I learned about French dirt the same way. Guess it never changes."

"Guess not."

"Spend any time in Japan?"

"After I was hit—yeah, a little."

"Meet any of them . . . you know" —and Gust would look to make sure Alice wasn't around, which was silly because she never bothered them once all the time Duda was there— "geisha girls?"

"Yeah, some; they're about average." Then Duda would take a sip. "But there *was* a girl I knew in Tokyo. . . ."

And he'd take off on a story about how he was in this place full of prostitutes, pretty drunk and with half his clothes off, and six or seven of these beautiful Japanese girls around him. But just about when it started to get interesting, if you know what I mean, Gust would look over at me and say, "Why don't you go ask Alice if maybe we shouldn't brew up a little ice cream, if she has salt and ice and some of those canned peaches. . . ."

"In a minute, Gust."

"*Move!*" Duda would cut in, without opening his eyes, and so I'd go because when Duda said it like that you just naturally went.

". . . pull the scarf out, you say?" That's what Gust was saying when I came back, though I'd run both ways. "Ha-*ha!* I bet *that* was something!"

But even though I didn't get in on the story, and no matter how many times I asked Duda later he never told me the part I missed, I can remember that picture like it was a photograph. Those two sitting on the porch and me down on the grass with the sun cooking us and then later cranking that ice-cream machine until it quit moving and eating sliced peaches wrapped in cold and gritty ice cream. I can still taste that ice cream when I close my eyes. . . .

Or another time when some of the cows started to come in season and we had to move the bull to the breeding pen. Like I said, bulls are always tricky, but never more than when the cows are coming in— the smell makes a bull go crazy—and just moving a bull from one pen to another can be awful hairy.

54

Just for no reason at all he can suddenly decide it's time to kill something.

Well, we had the bull out of one pen and halfway down this chute we'd rigged up leading to the breeding pen. Gust was twisting his tail to make him go and I'd turned around to close the gate in back so he wouldn't take it into his head to wheel around when he did just that—in that narrow chute he just kind of flipped end for end and started coming back for us, head down and tail up.

I figured we'd had it because there was no place to run in that chute and no time to climb over the side. We'd just stand there dumb while a long ton of Holstein ran us down and mashed us into the dirt.

But then Gust kind of shrugged all over and clasped his hands together like a club and raised them over his head and brought them down—just a little above the nose between the bull's eyes. Really *hard*—I mean it sounded like somebody squashing a rotten watermelon or something; ka-*chunk!* And the bull went down on his front knees like he'd been hit with a sledgehammer.

I thought he was dead. His eyes were rolled back so only the whites showed and his tongue stuck out the side and he was goobering spit by the quart. But Gust got down on his knees next to the bull's head and pulled his tongue out straight and started talking to him.

"Hey, bull," he said, in a really low, husky voice. "Dumb old bull, pulling that on *me*. Stupid old bull thinking you're going to run some people over and stomp a little. . . ." And he kind of ran the words all together so they didn't make much sense but sounded like singing, almost, or an Indian chant or something. It was the darnedest thing to hear, and pretty soon that old bull started to come around and his eyes moved back in the right place and he let out a sick bellow and Gust helped him get up.

Didn't take us but another minute or so to lead him back to the first pen, turn him around, and lead him to the breeding pen. Nice as a kitten all the way.

"Don't like to tap animals, generally," Gust said when we'd closed the gate. "They're doing what they think is right—it's like trying to make them play a game where they don't know the rules." He took out his tobacco can and took a dip, tucked it under his lip, and smiled. "He's a good old bull, that one. . . ." And he just stood there for a while and watched the bull smelling around the pen. Not like a man would watch an animal, but more like a man would watch another man; like they knew something about each other that was personal, almost a secret.

I didn't say anything. I was thinking, man, if that was just a tap, I didn't ever want to see Gust *hit* something. He'd probably tear it to pieces. And then I had a kind of just-pretend picture come into my mind, you know how you do, and I could see myself back in Gib's barn. Gib was taking down that trace chain and starting for me, and Gust just stepped in between and hit Gib like he hit the bull and just dropped him. It made me feel good, kind of warm, that thought—I had it several more times that week, until it more or less just slipped away, and every time it made me feel good to see it. I decided right then that I wanted to be like Gust when I grew up, but you know how fast that changes.

Other things happened that last month, other nice things. Like Alice crying when I chipped my tooth. It hurt like blazes and woke me up one night—I'd accidentally caught myself with the fork handle while cleaning the gutters one evening—and Alice came into my room and rubbed my hand and cried softly and said dumb things like "There, there, it'll be all right." It was nice even if I was thirteen going on fourteen, and sometimes later when things got bad I used to close my eyes and imagine Alice coming into my room and saying, "There, there, it'll be all right," and it made things a little better.

But pretty soon it was almost over. We had all the grain in, and Gust had done most of the fall plowing. School was due to start in a few days. It was something I didn't want to happen. I didn't want to go back to Twin Forks, or school, or home—I felt more at home at Gust's than I ever had with Mom and Dad—and I tried the tricks to make time go slower—counting minutes, watching the clock in the kitchen. I even did some things I didn't want to do, which always makes time go slow. I cleaned the pigpen even though Gust hadn't told me to do it, and cleaning a pigpen is the grubbiest thing in the world to get into; you stick a fork down in a whole summer's stored-up layer of pig manure, and when you break it sideways and open the crack, not even *flies* hang around. It's some rank smell, I'll tell you. But even that didn't help much, and finally it was the last day and we were waiting for Duda to come and get me. Even then I didn't give up but sat there watching down the driveway, wishing that maybe his car wouldn't start or he'd have two blowouts or throw a rod. . . .

"Well." Gust came out by the yard gate where I sat watching. "Ready to go back to the big city?"

I shook my head. There was a lump in my throat about as big as a basketball, and I didn't trust myself to speak. I made a thing out of getting up from where I hunkered and scuffed some dirt around the gatepost with my toe.

"Alice is inside," Gust said, "cooking, of course. Making something for you to take back with you."

I nodded.

"She does that when she gets upset. Cooks, I mean. Generally I don't do anything that foolish when something bothers me—I just get all red." He coughed. "Like now."

I looked up and sure enough, he was as red as beet pickles. I felt the lump start to come up and my eyes get all watery, so I looked away.

"Here's your pay." He handed me an envelope. "I tacked a bonus on for the pigpen. It was a good job."

"I did it to make the time go slower."

"Oh—well, still a nice job." He fished in his pocket and pulled out the tobacco. "Chaw?"

I shook my head and he filled his lip and put the round can back in his pocket.

"Should things go wrong . . ." he started, then stopped and rubbed the back of his neck. "I mean I suppose everything will work out all right at home for you. I just wanted you to know that if things go wrong or . . . well, what I want to say is it's been good having you around. Awful good."

Well, that did it. I just kind of busted up inside and the next thing I knew I was all mashed into his chest saying how much I didn't want to go home and crying and carrying on something perfectly *blubbery*. Would have made you sick to see it—just like a girl. But at the time it didn't feel wrong at all. I don't know how long we stood that way, probably only a couple of minutes, with Gust ruffling my hair and talking—saying nothing but in that same kind of low chant he used on the bull—when I heard a car and Duda came down the driveway.

I got my stuff and put it in the car. Duda didn't even get out but yelled to Gust he'd give him a visit sometime later. I opened the door and started to get in when Gust stopped me. "Alice," he said. "You gotta go get your stuff from her."

So I ran back into the house, still crying, and she was in the kitchen crying and had a big bagful of cookies and two pies and some cake. She gave me a hug that about squeezed the guts out of me, both of us bawling like kids—I never cried so much in my life, not even later—and I ran back outside and waved good-bye to Gust and jumped in the car and we drove on out.

Duda didn't say anything for two or three miles, just sat smoking while I sniffed and stared out the side window at the ditch. After a bit he shrugged. "Hey, kid, it's only eight miles from town—not like you're in the next state or something. You can come out and see 'em now and then. . . ."

"That isn't it."

"Yeah." He blew smoke at the windshield. "I know. . . ."

Which was the last thing we said until he pulled up in the driveway at Klein's grubby old apartment building.

Chapter Six

It was all right at home for a while, like it usually was when the welfare people or the law had had a run-in with my folks. They didn't stop drinking— they *never* stopped drinking, which is something I can't understand about some grown-ups.

I mean why is it that some of them, like Duda and Gust, can sit there and drink like they did that time at the farm and then stop and never get mean or scream or yell, and others are like my folks? It's like there's a fishhook in the bottle that gets caught in them somehow and when they start drinking they can't stop until they're drunk and mean and dumb. I've watched them hundreds of times and it's always the same. They get up and then they take a drink and there they go again—it's positively weird.

But when I came back from the farm, at least they weren't mean. They more or less went their way and I went mine and, like I said, for a while there it was all right. Along toward evening when they'd start to get loud and all, I'd go on out to the old Dodge and sit in there and read and then come back in when they'd passed out—usually about ten or eleven—and eat and go to bed on the roll-away bed I had in the corner of the living room.

School started, which wasn't too neat because I don't get along with other kids all that well. I mean they live a lot different from the way I do, if you know what I mean, so there isn't much for us to talk about. Like most of them have folks who get them gym clothes or, if they want to go out for hockey, good skates and gloves and all. Things like that I've pretty much got to buy my own, which most of the other guys know, like they know about my folks and the booze and everything, and so we just don't get along all that well. Except for Reggie Demars. I met him in bookkeeping and he became a pin setter in the alley next to me later and his folks are a lot like mine, but I'll talk more about that another time.

School pretty much bored me, what with having to be there and make classes—even though the typing teacher, Miss Peterson, was nice and pretty. The only reason I bring it up is because that's where I met Irene Johnson and fell in love—and that's what started all the trouble.

Irene was different from most of the other girls, I guess because she was new and hadn't had time to get all messed up the way the others were. Her folks had just moved to Twin Forks from Minneapolis, so they had big-city ways of doing things and thinking about life and all, so Irene was pretty neat.

Take how I met her, for example. We'd just gotten our lockers and hers was right across the hall from mine. Naturally she started having trouble with the combination lock on the thing—they never worked right—so when I saw that I went over to help her because she was cute and all. One thing led to another and I asked her if I could walk her home. Which is something I don't usually do, but you'd have to see her to understand. I mean standing there with her brown hair tied back in a ponytail and her sweater kind of flung back on her shoulders, leaning against the locker door so the full skirt she was wearing jutted out even more than it normally did—I mean she was something to see.

"Well," she answered me. "I guess so. . . ." And she looked like she was going to say something else, only Roger Haynes came up right about then and made his big move.

"Hi," he said, turning his back to me and facing Irene. "I saw you before around town. I'm Roger." He said it like he was saying he was God or something. "Can I walk you home after school?"

I mean Roger is one of the lucky ones. His folks

have money, so he gets all these neat clothes like white jeans with the buckle strap across the back and kind of loose loafers and a leather jacket with a fur collar. He's even kind of good looking, if you go for that sort of guy—tall, with a flattop that really stays flat and doesn't keep sort of wilting down like mine. I guess he's what you would call a good catch, especially for a new girl in town like Irene. But she turned him down.

"I'm going home with him," she said, pointing at me with a nod of her head. "He already asked me. . . ."

Which just goes to show you. I mean any of the other girls in school would have jumped at the offer and left me flat. Not Irene—she was different.

I don't really remember what we talked about that first day walking home. I guess maybe just school or something. I was embarrassed as all get out for a while, till we got out and away from the school a little. Joey Poole saw us and naturally said something he thought was funny and I got about as red as a beet and stayed that way until we got to Labrea Street, where Irene lived.

"Well," she said when we stopped at her door. "Thank you for walking me home."

"It was neat," I said, which I'll admit was pretty dumb, but all I could come up with at the moment. I forced myself to slouch and act like I was pretty cool about it all, the way you do, but my hands were a little sweaty so I jammed them in my pockets. "How about if I come by in the morning and walk you to school?"

"Sure," she nodded. "Why not?"

And that's how it started. It's funny, but thinking about it now after it's all over, it just doesn't seem that anything that could turn out that messed up could start so simple and easy. I guess that's how they all end up, though—the big love affairs. They begin just like any other relationship then somewhere along the line something changes and it all falls apart.

But that first afternoon when I walked home about four inches above the sidewalk it sure didn't seem like anything bad could *ever* happen to me again.

I was almost all the way home before it hit me; I needed clothes. I mean it was more than that—what with my going with Irene I had pretty much to change my whole life. But right off for the first time ever I had to face the fact that I *had* to get some nice clothes, to look good for Irene so she wouldn't feel bad being seen with me.

When I got back to the Dodge I dug out the rest of the money Gust had paid me from inside the front-seat cushions and headed for Penney's, where I walked through the best part of seventy dollars and kept buying right up until they closed at eight. But I was careful about it, and when I left I had enough clothes for the whole year—and the kind of clothes that would look nice with Irene. Like I got some white bucks, and even though they cost over five dollars—which is an awful lot for a pair of shoes, if you ask me—they were worth it. I mean when I put them on with black pants and the pink shirt there wasn't anybody in school, not even Roger Haynes,

65

that had shade on me for being neat and cool. I also got a leather jacket, black with a gray fur collar, and some new hair stuff that worked better than Butchwax. . . .

What I mean is, when I went by Irene's the next morning to walk her to school I was what you'd call a new man. And it wasn't wasted effort, either.

"You look different," she said, when she came outside. "Nicer."

I shrugged it off. "Just a few clothes." But inside I got warm and felt good all over. "It was about time for it."

I don't remember what we talked about on the way to school that morning, either, because all the way I was wondering what would happen if I just kind of casually reached out and brushed her hand with mine, like it was an accident, then sort of held it. . . .

Before I knew it we were at school, and there was Roger by her locker, so I had to make my move fast. "Walk you home this afternoon?" I tried to say it like it didn't matter, but it came out a little too fast.

"Well . . ." She was looking at Roger down the hallway. "I don't know. . . ." Then she sort of shrugged. "Sure, why not?"

And she did, too. Waited by her locker for me that afternoon and we walked home together again, and after the first block or two I finally worked up the guts to let my hand brush against hers and kind of catch and hold. She didn't even pull her fingers out of mine but just left them where they were and, man, if you don't think my heart was pumping like a motor or something!

When we got to her door, or actually a little before so her folks wouldn't see, I let go of her hand even though I didn't want to—I didn't want *ever* to let go. "How do you feel about scary movies?" I asked.

"Why?" She leaned back against the side of the door and looked so soft—kind of like Doris Day does in some of her movies—that I almost kissed her.

"The Forks is showing a really neat one Friday night." I jammed my hands in my pockets; they were getting sweaty again. "It's called *The Thing*. I thought maybe if you wanted to, I could kind of . . . I mean we could maybe go to the movie together."

"I'll have to ask my folks. . . ."

Which of course sounded like an excuse, so I tried to cover it the way you do. "Well, it was only an idea I had."

But she went in the house and a minute later came out. "They said it was all right. What time are you coming?"

Man! I almost passed out. "Six thirty? I mean the movie starts at seven, so I thought we should go early and get good seats."

"Sure."

I was almost all the way home before I remembered I hadn't asked her if I could walk her to school in the morning.

But it didn't matter. The next morning I just dropped by like I'd been doing it all my life and she

67

came out and we went to school. That afternoon her dad came and picked her up so I didn't get to walk her home. The next day was Friday so I didn't go by in the morning since we were going to the movie—I didn't want to push it all of a sudden.

The truth of the matter is that I was falling in love and I was afraid if I pushed it she would tell me to shove off.

Just shows you how dumb a kid can be. Now that I'm over fifteen and know what love is all about and everything, I can look back on it and see that it was just infatuation. But at the time it *felt* real, if you know what I mean—like I didn't think about Irene the way I thought about girls in magazines or the pretty typing teacher. With Irene it was different.

And all that Friday in school I don't think I did a thing right, just getting ready for that movie with Irene. I mean even in gym and shop the teachers nailed me—and how many things can you do wrong in shop, where all you're doing is making a plastic letter opener?

Six thirty just about *never* came. I stayed in the bathroom until almost six—Mom and Dad were drunk and fighting and I didn't want them to know I was going out, because when they were that way no matter what I wanted to do it was wrong and they wouldn't let me do it. Once, just to test it, I waited until they were pretty well soused and then told them I had to go see the minister about confirmation. Sure enough they wouldn't let me go—just out of meanness. So I stayed in the bathroom and worked on my hair until just before it was time to go. I must have worked about a pound of Butchwax into my flattop before it would stay up right, and then it wouldn't hold for more than a few minutes.

Finally I glommed a look at the kitchen clock and it was six and I slid out sideways while they were screaming and shagged it before they knew I was gone.

When I got to Irene's something happened that I can't understand to this day. I was afraid to knock on the door. I mean after all the excitement and waiting—like a date with Irene was the only thing I could *think* about—and I had to work up the guts to knock.

But when I finally did she came out and smiled, and as we started walking to the movie I knew that even if Joey Poole saw us and wisecracked like he always did I wouldn't blush.

I mean I had it made in the shade.

Chapter Seven

I don't know how other people feel about it, but as far as I'm concerned, if you want to get to know a girl fast—really break the ice and know *everything* about her—about the best thing you can do is take her to a really scary movie. It's something even grown-ups should think about—you see some of them the way they are, all fighting and screaming at each other, and it's clear as a bell they didn't know anything about each other in the first place or they would never have gotten married. . . .

Take this movie Irene and I went to, for instance. Like I said, it was called *The Thing,* and it was all about this ship from another planet landing up by the North Pole, where this monster gets frozen into a block of ice. So they find the monster in the ice and bring the whole block back to study it, but the very first night the guard who's watching it doesn't like the way it looks and covers the block with a blanket.

Wouldn't you know it? The jerk uses an electric blanket, and it's plugged in and melts the ice and thaws out the monster, which comes back to life and right away starts killing sled dogs and people because it lives on blood.

Man! There was one part in the movie where this guy opens a door and the monster is standing there waiting and it lets out a roar—every hair on the back of my neck jumped straight out and my guts turned into a knot.

And it was right then that I decided I loved Irene —didn't just like her a lot, but really loved her. The way you do.

I mean when that door opened and that big ugly thing stood up and let loose, Irene clamped around me so hard it almost broke my neck. And even though later things got a little sticky, I'll probably still love Irene that way until I die.

It was what you'd call my first real crack at hugging somebody of the opposite sex, unless you count aunts and cousins, and I don't mind saying that I liked it some. For the rest of the movie I kept my arm more or less draped across the back of Irene's seat, hardly sweating at all, and she even leaned back a couple of times so her ponytail was against my elbow, brushing it ever so lightly. . . .

I tell you if some people who get married would just take the time to go to a good scary movie before they tie the knot, there'd be a lot less divorcing and fighting going on in the world today. There's no way you can go through an experience like that without learning something about one another that you didn't know before. It just reaches down inside you and jerks it out.

The walk home after the movie was another thing I'll probably remember forever. It was dark, and I right away took her hand just like it was the most natural thing in the whole world. We had the after pictures from the movie in our minds, so we were still a little scared. I'll bet for a full block we didn't say anything—just walked holding hands. I don't know what Irene was thinking then, but I was all wrapped up in some pretty dumb stuff like what I'd do to save Irene if a monster came out from behind the hedge by Mrs. Kriel's house. I mean I had pictures of myself pushing Irene behind me, telling her to run—really *dumb*. Duda told me later that my brain had turned to mush, said it was fairly common with kids my age and even some grown-ups, and that it would more than likely go away when I got older. But I don't know because even now that I'm past fifteen, I can close my eyes and get the picture and feelings.

"That was sure a scary movie," Irene said, about halfway home. "Especially when they didn't know where the monster was and kept searching from room to room."

"Yeah." I mean that's *all* I said—a really whippy conversationalist. But for some reason when I heard her voice I started thinking about her lips and *that* got me to thinking about kissing her when I got her home, even though it was our first date. We'd walked to school and back a few times, and I was wondering if that didn't sort of count as dates, like maybe two walks to school and back were the same as one date, which meant we'd actually been on *more* than one date, and so it would be all right to try and kiss her good night if I could somehow work up the courage for it. . . .

Well, that naturally set my hand to sweating until it just poured, and *that* got me to worrying about what Irene would think about a guy who's supposed to be cool and neat and his hands are soaking wet, which made me forget about thinking about kissing her right when I'd just about decided to give it a shot.

Duda was right. Talk about your brain turning to mush—it felt like my whole head was made of jelly. Before I knew it we were at her house and she was ready to go in and I didn't remember half the walk home with her for worrying.

"Well." She stood there, the porch light catching the brown in her hair, flickering with the moths flying around the light, so pretty it just made me hurt inside.

"Yeah." I mean you'd have had to go at least a thousand miles to find somebody as dumb as I was that night.

"Thank you for taking me to the movie."

"It was nothing. . . ."

At that split second her chin moved up just the smallest part of an inch and her tongue came out and barely wet the left corner of her lips and jerked back in her mouth and her eyes half closed and I decided to give it a try.

It all sounds like I planned it or something. I didn't —it all happened so fast it was like falling down. One second we were standing like that just saying good night, and the next her chin moved and I just kind of let my head sag down a hair and put my lips on hers and it was over.

I'm not going to tell you it was a perfect kiss or anything like that. To be truthful, looking back on it, just before our lips met her head moved a little so it wasn't square on, but we had a good two-thirds contact, maybe a little more, and we held it like that for going on five or six seconds.

It maybe wasn't what you'd call a professional kiss, but it *was* a kiss, a real one, and it hit me just about like a hammer in the back of the head. She went in right after the kiss and I just stood there in the porch light, and if you'd asked me right then what movie we'd been to see, or my name, I couldn't have given you a straight answer.

I walked home, but I don't remember it except that I was singing something, which set the Larson's dog off to barking, which woke the Larsons, so I had to shag it past their house before they came out.

When I got home I decided not to go in. The folks were drunk again, or still, or whatever, and it somehow seemed that going into the apartment with those two screaming at each other and at me would have ruined the whole night.

So I curled up in the back seat of the Dodge and went to sleep and had a really screwy dream about Irene and *The Thing* and Gib Nymen. Gib and *The Thing* were after Irene and I was going to stop them, only I couldn't move fast enough, and just when it all looked really bad Duda showed up and called me a puke kid and saved Irene but wouldn't let me kiss her.

I mean it was a mess.

Chapter Eight

It's funny, not funny ha-ha, but funny weird, how when everything is over you can look back and see just how it could have gone right, how this little thing or that would have made all the difference.

Like if I hadn't fallen in love with Irene I wouldn't have needed money, and if I hadn't needed money I wouldn't have done anything wrong, and if I hadn't done anything wrong I wouldn't have gotten involved with Duda again, and if I hadn't gotten involved with Duda again he might still be alive. . . .

Duda would have called that stupid thinking, like thinking about what might have happened doesn't do any good. "That kind of thinking and a dime," he would have told me, "will get you a cup of coffee."

But it's true. And later it was the only kind of thinking I *could* do, stupid or not, and I wanted to run it all back to that one place and not kiss Irene on the porch the way I did, and not fall in love, and not . . .

Of course it wasn't all bad. Not at first. For the rest of that fall until late November it wasn't bad at all. In fact it was what you might call good.

Irene and I went to more movies, and kissed some more, and once I hugged her real tight—well, that doesn't matter. Let's just say things were going great. We weren't going steady or anything, but I think she was starting to fall for me the way I had fallen for her, which was pretty much head over heels, when I just flat ran out of money. Without money I couldn't date Irene, and if I couldn't date Irene I didn't figure life was worth living. So I had to get a job.

You ever try getting a job when you're fourteen, in school, live in a small town, and your parents are the town drunks?

It's *mean.* Somebody like Roger Haynes could just walk into the drugstore and twenty minutes later he'd be hired to jerk sodas, which he did, because his dad spends a lot of money in the same drugstore. Old Mr. Greshim, who owns the drugstore, probably even calls Roger "sir."

I walk into the drugstore and they think I'm going to steal something. They won't even let me go close to the magazine rack. That's how rough it is.

So I had two choices, both bad. I could sell papers around town, newspapers, hitting the bars and the hospital, which might make me a dollar every two days, which I did. And I was doing all right until they caught me on the maternity floor of the hospital, where I wasn't supposed to be, and I got fired.

Or you can set pins at Irv's bowling alley.

Which is a little like dying—or at least that's what Duda called it later that winter when I told him what it was like.

Just for starters the other guys back in the pits were the roughest guys in school. Except for Reggie Demars, who comes from a big family and works to help them eat and is a nice guy and a friend, the rest of them were just plain hoods. Levis so tight they could barely move in them, hair back in duck-tails with a lot of grease, and they all smoked. They were rough as cobs, as Duda would say, and Kenny Sova and Duane Peterson—the two meanest—decided my first night in the pits that they hated me.

The first night was tricky anyway. I'd never set pins before and could pick up only two pins at a time instead of four, which you can do when you learn to dislocate your thumb knuckles, and my timing was all wrong. Reggie showed me how to work the machine—he was working the alley on my right side, Kenny Sova the one on my left. The way it worked—getting down, throwing the ball into the ball-return slot first so it would roll back, picking up the pins and slamming them into the machine, and then getting back up onto the bench before the bowler threw his next ball—took just about everything out of me.

I got hit once when a bowler threw before I could get out of the way—the ball just grazed my leg—and I would have been clobbered really hard in the head once when I bent over if Reggie hadn't screamed "Ball!" in the nick of time, which is the warning you yell if another setter doesn't see it coming.

Pits is a good word for what it's like when you set pins. It's dark back there, and hot and stinky from the sweat that pours out of you. You bend and stretch and bend and stretch and slam the wooden pins into the machine and duck when they go flying off the back cushion. And the noise from that sixteen-pound bowling ball thundering into those four-pound hickory pins again and again makes your head hurt and your ears almost bleed.

Pretty soon there is nothing in the world but your pit. It's all you know—bending and stretching and throwing, over and over again, sweating and trying to catch your breath. It isn't bowling anymore, it isn't a game; it's just you and the balls and the pins and you aren't really alive, like Duda says, and you aren't really dead. You're just setting pins.

For four hours every night.

And that first night I could think only about somehow making it, staying alive until eleven, when the leagues would be finished for the night and I would be able to go home and go to bed and never get up.

I had just reached over to throw the ball into the ball-return rack when Kenny Sova took a piece of coat-hanger wire and wrapped it around my neck from the rear and twisted it once so it stayed tight and choked me.

It happened that fast. I didn't know *what* was going on, only that I was choking to death. The next thing I knew I was down on my knees and Reggie jumped from his pit into mine and took the wire off and I pulled breath like a snagged sucker on the bank.

"They play rough," Reggie said, jumping back into his own pit just in time to return a ball and set a strike. "Don't let them get away with it, or they'll never let up on you."

I turned and Kenny and Duane were laughing like they'd just pulled the joke of the century or something, so I flipped Kenny the bird and went back to setting.

I didn't get my chance for almost a whole line, which really gave me time to work up a mad, the kind that comes right before you cry, when you have plenty of time to think about it. Finally Kenny stopped watching me so close. He got into setting pins, and I waited until he was coming up with both hands full of pins and his back to me.

With no warning, no sound, not even a grunt, I took a pin and hit him so hard on the top of his duck-tailed head that it turned his teeth to powder.

He went down like the bull Gust had hit and for a minute I thought I'd killed him, but then he started breathing—jerky, but breathing—and I went back to setting pins and figured that was the end of it.

Which was a mistake.

I had to fight Kenny every night before we set pins for the rest of the winter as long as I worked in the bowling alley. And when I quit setting pins he'd catch me after school and we'd go around for a while, and when I started trying to find new ways to get home he'd lay for me in the hallways during school. It finally got to the point where if I even *saw* Kenny I'd just get ready for it because as sure as God made apples, Kenny was going to tear into me. Not only was he mean and dumb, but Kenny Sova has *got* to be the stubbornest person in the world, and I'll bet I hold the world record for black eyes and split lips. I haven't looked what you'd call normal since that night when I hit him with the pin and it's been over a year now. And while it's too soon to tell for sure, it's likely that if I make it to thirty or forty years old and happen to meet Kenny on the street, I'll still have to fight him.

But the worst thing about setting pins was that it didn't solve my problem. I made a little money—in a good week, with tips, we could make close to fifteen bucks—but I had to work every night.

Which meant that while I was working to make money to be able to see more of Irene I couldn't see more of Irene because I never had any free time because I was working to make money to be able to see more of Irene. . . .

It was what Duda called the monkey-chasing-its-tail merry-go-round, which he said a lot of grown-ups did. They seemed to be working all the time just to be able to make money and never had any free time to do what they'd like to do, like fish or hunt. "It's easy to get on it," he told me once while we were driving around, "and once you're on it you can't get off." Then he smiled, that sideways smile that wasn't really meant to be funny, and said, "I never got on it." Which wasn't really true, since he was working almost all the time as a cop. But it's what he said, and even if he was wrong about his not being on it, once you get caught up in it it's a bear to get loose. For sure.

But looking back on it, the way you do, what really gets me down about it all is that while I was getting caught on the merry-go-round trying to solve the problem of seeing more of Irene, Roger Haynes turned fifteen and got his driver's permit and his dad bought him a car.

It wasn't much of a car—just a crummy old 1946 Ford—but it ran, and don't you know the first thing Roger did was make this big move on Irene. Naturally she picked up on it because Roger had both money *and* a car—not to mention plenty of free time since he was working days and late afternoons only, jerking soda at Greshim's—and the next thing I knew I was walking down the street one day and Roger and Irene go flipping by like nobody's business.

I couldn't blame Irene, really. I mean there was Roger, who isn't ugly, and he had a car and money and all. What girl wouldn't take that rather than a pin setter with no car and a busted-up face?

And there was no way to know then that Irene's going with Roger would lead me into a life of crime.

Chapter Nine

Broken hearts are strange things. When I first saw Irene with Roger I thought I'd die. I mean really die. Everything seemed to be so wasted all of a sudden, all the work and worry and the movies—which sounds dumb but didn't at the time—and time and walks and holding hands and sweating and setting pins.

All for nothing. That's how it felt when I saw them drive by. Like all I was or ever would be was right then for *nothing*, and if I hadn't been so afraid of booze because of what it did to my folks I think I would have started drinking.

What I did instead was throw myself into my work. I became, according to Irv, who owned the bowling alley and ought to know, the best damn pin setter who ever came down the pike. Normal setters can pick up four pins at a time, two in each hand, but I found that by dislocating the knuckles of not just the thumb but of the little finger as well I could pick up *six* pins—three in each hand.

I started setting two alleys at once, going back and forth between them, and doubled my weekly earnings, and once in a while, because I was getting into shape from all the work, just once in a while, when Kenny and me would get into a knuckle-duster, I'd come out on top.

I'd like to say I forgot about Irene, that I got into my work and other things so much that she didn't matter, that I used all the money I was making for something sensible—I mean, I was raking down close to thirty cool ones a week, almost a fortune.

But I didn't. I didn't forget about Irene because I saw her almost every day in school, walking around with Roger because they were going steady—or at least she was wearing his ring around her neck on a chain—and I didn't do anything with the extra money except spend it on junk. Clothes, shoes, engineer boots, a hunting coat made out of canvas with a really neat pocket across the back for dead birds, two new belts (the thin black kind)—it got so every time I walked into Penney's everybody in the store smiled. I just bought and bought and bought. Irv paid us on Saturday morning, and I was broke by noon every Saturday, and it went like that for over a month, which is a long time when you're setting pins and fighting all the time and walking around with a broken heart.

I saw Duda once or twice during that month, just driving by, and Mom and Dad got to drinking really heavy again during the same month. Dead winter came and a kid named Zavorall fell through the ice and drowned. They didn't find his body for almost a week during that month, and when they did find it, washed out from the bottom of the dam spillway, the fish had been at it and they wouldn't let his mother see the body—though I got a look at it before they got it in the rubber bag and it was pretty bad. All of that happened during that month and none of it sticks in my memory as much as one phone call at the end of that month.

Usually nobody called me, so I didn't bother to answer the phone very often. So this day when it rang I was out in the Dodge reading a Western. Mom screamed at me through the hole in the corner of the kitchen window where she'd thrown an ashtray once when she was drunk and stuffed it full of news-paper.

It was Irene on the phone.

"How are you doing?" she asked.

Which really threw me. I mean I sure hadn't forgotten her, but I was almost certain she'd forgotten all about me, what with Roger and his money and car and flattop that stayed flat and all.

"Oh, you know. All right, I guess." which was a flat lie. I wasn't doing all right at all.

"What are you doing tonight?"

"Uhh . . . nothing," I forced my brain into action. "Why?"

"Oh, I was just thinking maybe we could get together." Her voice sounded tight, like she was working hard to control it.

"What about Roger?" Right, I thought, put your foot right smack in the *middle* of your mouth. "I mean I thought you and Roger were, well, going pretty regular . . ."

"That's over."

"Oh."

"So I thought maybe you could come over and pick me up and we could go for a walk and talk a little. . . ."

"Well, sure." I was trying to remember if I had enough Butchwax to bring my hair up one more time. "When should I come?"

"Six o'clock?"

"See you then."

Actually I got there a little before six, maybe two minutes early, but she'd been watching out the door window and came out even though I was early. It was dark—in the winter it gets dark just after four in Twin Forks—but even in the poor light I could see that she'd been crying, so I just took her hand and we walked down Labrea, breathing the cold air. I didn't say anything and she didn't talk for quite a while. I started feeling strange, wondering what I was doing here walking down a cold street with Roger's ex-steady and not saying a word. I was just going to stop and say something, *anything* to break the silence, when she did it for me.

"The reason I wanted to talk to you"—she stopped and looked up at me— "is that I want to get married."

"Uhhh . . . I see." I looked up at the streetlight. There was a blue ring around it from the cold.

"To you."

It didn't register at first. I was still looking up at the blue ring and I noticed that it seemed to swell like an expanding halo or something as the ice crystals in the air moved. "Unnnhh . . . to *me?*"

"Yes—oh, darn, I'm not doing this right." She started crying. "I was going to play this right and get you to . . . and it's not working. The truth is that I have to get married."

"Have to?"

She nodded, sobbing. "I'm pregnant."

"But . . . pregnant. Isn't that . . . well, I mean if you're pregnant it must be that somebody else . . . that is, shouldn't the person who made you pregnant be the one who marries you?"

"Roger. It was Roger and he won't marry me, or maybe he will, but I don't want to marry him. I want to marry you."

Which was all right for a while. I mean the way she said it. Maybe I was only fourteen and it wasn't me that had made her pregnant and maybe it was all pretty stupid-sounding—but, man, it was all right there for just a little while. I couldn't stop my thinking and it all rolled together—setting pins and the kiss and Irene crying and the dream I'd had that night after the movie and the feeling of wanting to protect her and loving her or at least thinking I loved her, which was the same thing. And now she wanted to marry me and not Roger, even though he had a good flattop and a car and money. . . .

I mean just for a little, not long, but at least for long enough to get to feel that the world was all right.

And then I went crazy and became a criminal and maybe worse and it all fell apart.

Chapter Ten

The whole problem was that you can't support a wife and kid, even if the kid isn't yours, on just what you make setting pins. I needed money, lots of it, maybe fifty or sixty dollars to start with and more later because I really loved Irene and wanted to marry her and take care of her and protect her and be with her forever.

Which all sounds dumb now, but the feelings were real then, or I wouldn't have done what I did.

I didn't set out to do anything really illegal to get

money, like steal something somebody wanted. But old Mrs. Kriel had lost both her husband and her son on a fishing trip and she'd kept all their gear in her garage for years and years and didn't even really know it was there anymore. I'd seen it through the window once and there was a lot of neat stuff—fishing outfits and hunting knives and guns and packs. I mean they'd been a real outdoors family.

What I figured was that since she didn't know what was there anyway I could kind of borrow some of the junk and sell it and pick up some money.

Which is stealing—only not really, if you know what I mean. Like if you've *got* to do something wrong, isn't it best to pick the least wrong thing you can do? I mean it's not like I was going to knock over a bank or something. Most of that stuff would have just rotted anyway, sooner or later.

So I waited until a no-moon night in January after I'd finished setting pins. It was so cold you could make water and lean on it, as they say in Twin Forks, and I made a run on Mrs. Kriel's garage.

There was a padlock on the door facing the alley, but the screws on the hasp were exposed and I'd brought a small screwdriver—I mean I had it *planned* —and I was down to the last screw when the lights hit me.

"Freeze, maggot meat!" I recognized Duda's voice right away. "Up against the wall!"

Somehow he'd cut the engine on the prowl car and coasted off the street up behind me without making any sound. Then he'd hit the lights and I was pinned like a butterfly.

So I leaned up against the wall, you know the way they do in the movies, with my hands out, and he walked up behind me.

"The puke kid." He stood in back of me so I couldn't see him. "It figures. Got anything to say for yourself before I take you in?"

I shrugged, which isn't all that easy when you're leaning against a wall. "I wasn't doing anything wrong. . . ."

He hit me so hard I slammed into the wall and my nose started to bleed. "Don't lie, puke. You were breaking into this garage, I *know* that; now you want to tell my why?"

I couldn't, of course—tell him, I mean—so I stood there looking at the ground, watching the blood drip from my nose and splash in the frozen snow and freeze. It looked black in the headlights.

"Get in the car."

I started for the front seat.

"*Back* seat, in the cage."

So I got in back and sat there waiting while he closed the doors and I *was* in a wire cage, with the mesh across between the back and front seats and the door and window handles removed. It wasn't like riding up front, I can tell you, and I started thinking like a criminal right off, wondering what the judge would do and how much time I'd get and thinking how I wouldn't see Irene for a long time, probably. The next thing I know I was bawling like a new calf, sitting in the wire cage with tears running from my eyes and blood from my nose and my whole life ruined.

93

It was pretty disgusting, and the more I tried to stop, the worse it got.

Duda got in front and started up the car and took off down the alley. We'd gone maybe four or five blocks when I realized through my misery that we weren't heading in the direction of the jail but going the opposite way, heading for the edge of town.

"Where we going?" I asked.

He didn't answer and I didn't repeat the question. I might be pretty blockheaded, but it was getting through to me that when you dealt with Duda you didn't want to push anything. Besides, Twin Forks isn't that big and in no time at all we'd cleared the city limits and were heading north up the highway that leads to Middle River, only Middle River was thirty miles away and when Duda had driven ten miles he stopped the car.

"Out." He rolled down his window and reached around outside to open my door.

"What?"

"Out of the car."

"Here?" I looked around through the open door. It was at least ten below and there was nothing, I mean *nothing* between here and town for ten miles. "What for?"

"You want me to dribble you like a basketball?" His voice got hard. "Get out of the car."

So I got out and stood alongside the black-and-white patrol car with my head jammed down in the fur collar of my leather jacket—because it wasn't cool to wear a hat and ruin your flattop—and my hands crammed in my pockets.

"Way I figure it is this way," Duda said, and damned if he didn't smile. "I take you in and the judge will probably put you on probation, the way he does with other puke kids, and you don't get anything out of it except once a week you have to talk with the probation officer, who has thirty or forty other kids to talk to anyway. What you really need is time to think, not all that mess with the probation officer. So you start walking, right in front of this car, and all the way back to town you think how *stupid* it was to break into that garage, right?"

I nodded.

"And if you stop, or if I just *once* find myself wondering if you're still thinking about how stupid you are, if for just the tiniest part of a second your mind wanders, puke kid, I am going to stop this car and get out and you *know* what happens if I stop and get out, don't you?"

I didn't, but I could guess. "You're going to whup up on me?"

"They will be able to bury you in a shoebox." He lit a cigarette and spit out the window onto the icy road. "For you have messed with the bull, boy, and he who messes with the bull gets the horn. Now start walking."

It was just a shade over ten miles back to town, and while that might not seem so far, let me tell you that when it's ten below and you're walking in front of a squad car and the road is icy, it's far enough to think maybe you're the stupidest person in the whole world for trying to break into a garage. I'm not certain how long it took, probably two or three hours at least, maybe even four, and about every fifteen minutes Duda would roll his window down and rub it in.

"Warm in here. Nice night for a ride. Care to get in and tell me why you were breaking into that garage?"

And I'd keep walking, breathing my own steam, listening to the engine running in back of me and the slow crunch of the tires on the road. I was sure mad at Duda, of course, but I was more mad at myself, and I was crying and kicking the ground while I walked—you know the way you do—and I swore a little and I guess I was almost all the way back to town when I decided to tell Duda the whole story.

I mean it didn't happen that fast. I've never had a lot of luck talking with grown-ups, what with my folks and judges, but as I walked I kept thinking that it was wrong for Duda to think I had just been breaking into a garage without a reason. After his helping me out of that Trontvet mess and getting me a job with Gust and all, it didn't seem right to just let him believe I was really only another rotten kid.

When I could see the lights of Twin Forks a mile or two ahead, I stopped and heard the car stop behind me. Duda didn't say anything as I walked back and got into the front seat next to him, but he offered me a cigarette, which was nice, and I almost took it except that I didn't smoke. I was sniffling a little and he let me get collected while he drove slowly back into town.

"You in some kind of trouble, kid?" He smiled and it was a real smile.

"Yeah. Well, not really, but sort of." I wiped my nose with the back of my sleeve and was surprised to see blood come off. I'd completely forgotten about the nose bleed. "There's this girl. . . ." I couldn't get it out.

"There are lots of girls, kid. The world's full of them."

"This one is pregnant." I darn near spit it.

"Ahhh." He turned to me. "Man, when you make a mess, you really do it *right*, don't you? You're what, fourteen? And you got some girl in trouble?"

"*I* didn't do it. . . ."

"Sure."

"No, really. It was Rog . . . it was this other guy. But I'm in love with the girl and she doesn't want to marry the other guy, and I want to marry her but I needed money to support a wife and kid."

He stared at me for a full minute, I mean we almost went off the road, and then finally shook his head. "You're telling the truth, aren't you?"

I nodded. "And that's why I broke into—I mean tried to break into the garage. Not because I'm a puke kid but because I needed the money to support a wife and baby."

He looked at me again. "I don't believe this, don't believe you. Either you are the dumbest little runt ever born, which is just possible, or the most addlepated, misguided piece of screwed-up thinking to hit Twin Forks since the beginning of time." He snorted and threw his cigarette out the wind-wing. "That or you're plain crazy."

I waited. There didn't seem to be much else to do.

"Lord. Don't you know *anything?*"

"Well, yeah, some things . . ."

"About life?"

"I guess not. . . ."

He looked at his watch, one of those big jobs with numbers and dials all over it—I found out later he took it off a dead Chinese he killed in Korea—and shrugged tiredly. "I get off in ten minutes, at four in the morning. You wait in my own car and we'll go out and try shoot a few rabbits and I'll tell you the facts of life."

Which didn't need an answer, so I just leaned back in the seat and let him drive.

Chapter Eleven

And that's really how it all started, how I came to
live in the back of the squad car, which isn't really
all that much different from an old Dodge, and how
I got to know Duda and Twin Forks. Every night
when I'd quit setting pins Duda would be cruising
and he'd pick me up and we'd drive around, and
when he'd get off at four we'd go out and shine rabbits—you could get a buck for jackrabbits then because they used them for mink food—and sometimes
fox and wolves.

Well, every night except a few we did that. Some nights, of course, other things came up.

Like that first night. I waited in Duda's old Chrysler while he went in and changed shifts and clothes, and he came out wearing the same leather jacket that he wore with his uniform but different pants and shirt.

It took ten minutes or so to get out of town, heading north again, and he didn't say anything until we were a mile past the town-limits sign.

"Let me tell you about ovens," he said, then, smiling.

"Ovens?"

"Yeah. Like when it's somebody else's biscuit in the oven it's *his* bread when it comes out, not yours."

"Oh. Well, yes, I can see that—but this is different."

"The devil it is. Listen, numbnuts, you're only fourteen. Don't take more than you need to take. They're going to dump things on you later so heavy and so fast, you'll be lucky to take it—a lot of people don't."

"You mean like Carl Sunstrom?"

"Yeah. I mean like Carl—a casualty of war."

"I didn't know he was hit."

"He wasn't. Carl is a different kind of casualty. Like me. . . ." He trailed off and stared out the windshield. "Like me." He shook his head like there was something stuck to it he didn't like, and of course I didn't know what he was talking about then and didn't find out until later how even though Duda didn't drink like Carl, they were both casualties.

"Just don't take more than you have to take, kid,"

he repeated, and I think he was going to say more, except that a jackrabbit cut out of the ditch and ran down the road between the headlights and I had to get the shotgun out of the back seat and load it.

The rabbit stayed on the road, the way they do, and Duda slowed down to keep it in front of us between the lights until I got the double-barrels closed again and pointed out the partially opened door.

I'd never fired a shotgun before, just .22 rifles, so I wasn't ready for it and the kick about tore my shoulder loose when I cut down on the rabbit because I pulled both triggers at once and fired both barrels instead of just one.

Bits of rabbit cartwheeled and splattered down the road and blood and guts went everywhere and my ears were ringing when Duda stopped the car, so I didn't hear his breathing until later, when I got used to the gun and didn't shoot more than one barrel.

"Hey, kid, you tore him to shreds."

"Sorry." And I *was*, too, my shoulder hurt like blazes. "I didn't mean to pull both triggers. . . ."

Duda was standing over the rabbit, so I left the car, which he'd stopped right after I shot, and went over to him. The rabbit was still twitching, its mouth opening and closing a little, the eyes getting glazed. The charges had taken him right in the middle and the whole center of him was gone, just gone, and I didn't like it much, standing there looking at him. It was like we were seeing something we shouldn't see, and then I looked up at Duda.

He was staring at the rabbit's head. "*Watch—*

watch the life fly from his eyes, go out and out and out until it's gone. Don't you ever wonder where it goes?"

I mean it didn't even sound like Duda. His voice was low and husky and it was like I wasn't there, like it was only Duda and the rabbit dying there on the road, or already dead and twitching.

It scared the life out of me, is what it did, and sometimes now when the dreams come bad and I can't get to Bonnie to talk because she's busy the rabbit and Duda get all mixed up together somehow. Just that first rabbit comes into the dream, that first rabbit and Duda, even though we killed maybe hundreds of them—it's that first one that I pulled both triggers on that sticks in my mind, and the way Duda looked at it, and the cold night and the smell of its blood all over the icy road.

When the rabbit quit twitching we picked it up and threw it in the trunk and kept driving. I killed three more rabbits that night, which made me think about giving up setting pins, since I could make more hunting with Duda, but then I remembered Irene and decided to do both. Maybe I'd have enough money after all to get married and support a baby. That lasted until Duda opened up again.

"I get the money from the rabbits," he said, "all of it. You get guidance."

So much for that. "Well, if I'm going to get guidance, what should I do about this mess I'm in?"

"You have to ask?"

"Well." I moved my shoulders inside my coat. "I love her, you know."

"Yeah." He said it like he might say "bull." "With all your heart, right?"

I nodded.

"And you'll just *die* if you lose her, right?"

I nodded.

"Lord."

"That doesn't help. . . ."

"Don't be wise."

"Sorry."

"Look, do me a favor." He looked at me on the other side of the car seat. "Just don't do anything about it for a week or two, all right? I'll pick you up when you get done setting pins and we'll drive for a while and talk and hunt some more and maybe it'll wear off. If that doesn't work . . ."

I waited. "What?"

He shifted into second as we came into town and the sun made the sky gray. "If that doesn't work I'll knock some sense into you."

Chapter Twelve

I think it was working right when things went crazy
that night, when things turned upside down.

I mean I'd see Irene in school, of course, and she'd
ask me how it was going in that way she'd ask when
she really wanted to be asking me something else.
Her condition didn't show, at least I couldn't see it,
and I played it like Duda had said and just didn't say
or do anything except tell Irene I was busy setting
pins and making as much money as I could. Which
was the truth but not all of it, because I was doing

more than setting pins. I was learning about Twin Forks, and hunting, of course, but mostly about Twin Forks.

You see a town in the day and it's one thing, with all the stores open and people moving around and living going on. It's like that sign when you drive into Twin Forks and the friendly folks welcoming you and all—that's the daytime Twin Forks.

At night it's different.

"Day is the meat," Duda told me once while we were driving around. "It's the soft, fleshy part, the part everybody sees, the part you can clean and make pretty and turn into something it isn't. Day is the phony part of the town, the part to sleep through."

"And night?" Nights had always scared me, nights when Mom and Dad got drunk and fought, nights when it got dark and I was alone in my room and alone in the house and alone in the whole world. Nights were never good to me.

"Nights are the skeleton of a town," he said, wheeling the squad car around the back of Jung's bakery and down the alley. "The bone, and as everybody knows, the closer the bone, the sweeter the meat. You can't hide a town at night—it's real, alive, and honest. That's why I've always worked night shifts and always will. . . ."

But I think it was for other reasons. I mean maybe Duda was right about the nights, and for sure I found out a lot I wouldn't have found out during the daytime, but at night Duda could see Bonnie Wegee, who lived on the south side of the river and was one of those women who understand men a lot, if you know what I mean.

And I think Duda liked nights because it was the time when he was with people he knew best, although he'd probably get mad at that because he liked to think he knew everybody well. But he didn't know day people the way he knew people who came out when the sun went down. Like during the day he would probably have to talk to old Mr. Greshim, who owned the drugstore, and people like that made Duda stand funny, not loose, and change his voice to make it more polite. He wasn't Duda during the day, he was what people wanted him to be—the courteous cop. But at night he would go into the back of Johnny's hamburger shop, where they were running the poker game. Dr. Bradduck would be one of the people playing, Dr. Bradduck who went to church and talked about doing good all the time, and Duda would stand loose and maybe drop three or four words the way he did when he was being Duda, all hard and crisp, and pick up his take from the game and leave.

"No bull," he told me the first night when he came out with money from Johnny's. "During the day I'd have to call him "Doctor," be phony; but at night he's just another cat."

And we'd go to Bonnie's, where Duda would go in and stay a long time, sometimes two hours, while I sat in the car and listened for any calls on the radio. Once while I was sitting like that, waiting, Bonnie came out with a plate of leftover chicken and some milk. She was wearing a housecoat that was partially open and when she leaned over to hand me the chicken I could see why Duda liked to spend so much time with her. She was awfully pretty, almost as pretty as Irene, and she smelled like a woman should smell—soft, warm and a little musty at the temples.

I found out that Duda was married, and once, just once while we were driving around, I was thinking of Irene and Bonnie and Duda all mixed up and I asked Duda about his wife.

"She's a day person," he'd answered, and his voice sounded like rusty razor blades.

"Oh."

"It happens like that sometimes."

"Oh."

"Day people and night people getting together. It happens."

"I see." But I really didn't and only knew that Duda didn't want to talk about it, so I never asked again but found out one night in the pits that Duda's wife was really straitlaced and wouldn't have any kids and that they had what is known as a bad marriage.

I guess if you really pin it down I didn't learn so much about just Twin Forks riding around with Duda as I learned about Duda *and* Twin Forks, and mostly just about Duda. That was all right because I never really had a father except for the one who is drunk all the time, and since Duda was there and handy, I just started thinking of him a little like that. As a sort of father. And it's a good thing to know your sort of father, isn't it? Unless, of course, something happens to him the way it did to Duda, but that was later and I didn't know it was going to happen.

Like I really thought Duda was hard and tough and mean, but there was this one night we were cruising the alley in back of the Mint Bar and found Carl sitting drunk next to a garbage can holding his green wine bottle and puke all over his flight jacket. It would have gagged a maggot.

Duda got out of the car and I thought he was going to run Carl in, but he didn't. Instead he took out his handkerchief and squatted down in front of Carl and started wiping the vomit off his jacket, talking low and soothing while he wiped.

"Ahh, Carl, this isn't any good, you know we have to try and come back even when we can't because that's the only thing there is for us. . . ."

And it wasn't what he said so much as the way he said it, like music, like when Gust talked to the bull he'd knocked down. Pretty soon he had Carl all cleaned up and got him to his feet and helped him to the car and we took him back to his room across from the Catholic school where he sometimes janitored. And when Duda came back out from the room his nose was running and his eyes were wet, which isn't normal for a tough guy.

"You got something to say?" He slammed the door on the patrol car harder than usual.

"Nope."

"Good. Keep it that way."

Which I did, of course, because when his voice was like that you didn't want to say *anything*.

And another time we were cruising in back of the liquor store when we saw this guy trying to walk down the alley and he was so drunk he'd wet his pants, wet down to his knees, and he was just sliding along the wall, kind of clawing himself along. It was my dad.

"Ahh, kid, I wish you didn't have to see this," Duda said, and I knew he meant it.

"I see it all the time. At home."

"I know. But out here . . . out here it's different somehow. Like you're not supposed to see this part of it, only the part at home."

And I knew exactly what he meant, which surprised me some, and I sat and cried to myself for a while as we drove past Dad. But it was crying for Dad, and not because I was feeling sorry for myself, because I wasn't supposed to know this about Dad and now I knew it and would always know it.

Another time we were hunting and I stood up in the open car door to shoot a fox, and I got him, only the kick of the shotgun knocked me loose and I fell out of the car, which was doing about thirty miles an hour, and tumbled end over end down the road.

Duda was there next to me. He had stopped the car and was by my side before I'd finished rolling, practically, and he was almost like a mother, the way Alice had been that day at the farm.

"You all right? You okay?" he asked. "Fool kid dumping off the car like that. What got into you, doing something that dumb?"

And the words rolled together in that music and he touched my cheek where it had been cut by the stock of the shotgun when I fell. It wasn't like Duda at all, but like somebody else, maybe a sort of father.

Two minutes later we were back in the car and it was like it had never happened. He was his gruff old self.

But it *had* happened, and it wasn't something a tough guy does, and it's the part of Duda I remember now when the dreams come down hard.

Yet I saw Duda mean, too, and that was part of him, only looking back I don't think it was his fault. Just something war had made him into, like it had turned Carl into a wino.

One night we got called to where a man and his wife were having a fight—what cops call a domestic disturbance, the worst part of police work. When we got there Duda made me stay in the car, which he always did when there might be trouble, and went up to the back door.

At the second knock or so the door opened and a shotgun barrel came out and tucked itself under Duda's nose. I mean it happened that fast; I could see it from the car. So Duda just kind of moved his head sideways a little and the gun went off and missed but left a powderburn on the side of his cheek.

111

Man! He reached into that doorway and pulled the guy out onto the back porch and started beating on him, screaming and kicking him in the face.

It was like Duda went nuts, wild crazy.

"You son of a bitch trying to kill me!" he screamed, and he took his club out and half killed the guy before he'd cooled down.

But then he didn't arrest him, he just left him on his own back porch, all busted up and bleeding. When he got in the car he didn't say anything and we drove away like it had never happened.

"That guy tried to kill you," I said, when we'd gone about half a block.

"Naw. He's just messed up a little."

"Your face is burned."

"I'll live."

"You aren't going to arrest someone who half takes your head off with a shotgun, and you were going to throw *me* in the clink for taking some screws out of an old garage door?"

"You got something else you want to say?"

"Well, no. Since you put it that way."

"Good. Then shut up."

"Sorry."

"It's all right. Just don't talk so much." He adjusted his harness to make it more comfortable for sitting. "You talk *all* the time."

And then he broke into a really dirty song about an Indian maid in a shack who wasn't afraid. I won't put it all in here because I'm not sure it's proper, but he had at least four hundred songs like that, right down and grubby, and he'd sing them all the time when he was thinking. And he had a poem that at least once a night he'd say:

> "Up my nose,
> down my spine.
> Won't you be
> my Valentine?"

Which he would sometimes sing but mostly just whisper, and once when I asked him where it came from he told me a friend in Korea had used it one night for a password and it had stuck in his mind.

"I may not join the Army," I told him. "Not if it's all like that."

"Whatever gets you through the night." He laughed. "But if they want you, they got you, boy."

I mean he could be all light and quick like that, flipping out words like cards off the top of the deck, just minutes after almost beating the life out of that guy on the porch.

He'd go from hard to soft and back to hard so fast, you couldn't keep up sometimes, the way he would slide around, and I think maybe that was why when we ran into the bank robbers and he did what he did, it upset me and caused me to sin—*really* sin, not Gib Nymen sin—the way I did.

Or think I did. Sometimes it gets mixed up with the dreams.

Chapter Thirteen

Sometimes you forget things, big things you do or see or are because remembering them hurts so bad you don't want to bring them out.

Once Duda and I were driving out to the golf course to check on a barking dog, which we didn't find—you never find them—and I asked him why Carl Sunstrom drank wine all the time and didn't seem to want to pull himself out of it even though he seemed to be a pretty sharp guy. "Like he said, he knew you because people like him always knew cops, which is a sharp thing to say, right? I mean the way he put it. . . ."

Duda seemed to get mad at me for asking. "People like you, runt, haven't even got the right to *ask* about people like Carl."

"I've got to learn."

"Hummph!" He lit a cigarette, driving with one hand. "Yes. I suppose you do."

"So why does Carl drink like that when he isn't like my folks? Why doesn't he get mean drunk the way they do and doesn't seem to get hooked the same way?"

"Because your folks drink to get away from something they don't understand. Maybe each other. And Carl drinks to forget something he understands too well."

"What's that?"

"War."

"Well, yeah, but a lot of people went to war and they don't drink to forget it. You. Gust Homme. Like that."

"Well, there's war and there's war, and there's people and there's people. Me and Gust, we just more or less kept ourselves from getting shot up, which is mostly what you do in war."

"And Carl?"

"Carl had to do something worse, or at least something he considered worse than normal."

"What?" I mean I couldn't let that one go by.

"Never mind. It was just bad. According to his own rules, and they're the only rules that count.

116

Don't ever forget that—sometime between midnight and morning, when it's dark, you're going to be alone, and whatever you did or didn't do by your own rules, your own mind, your own thinking, will be all that counts. And if you did something wrong by those rules, you might wind up drinking to forget."

"Have you ever done anything like that?"

"Yeah."

"What?"

"Don't push it, runt." He glanced at me. "Don't push it."

"Why don't you drink? I mean if you had to do something you consider wrong, like Carl did something he thought was wrong, how come you don't drink like Carl?"

"There are other ways to forget. I just use another way."

"What way is that?" I was thinking that since I couldn't drink, if I ever needed a way to forget, maybe Duda's way would work, but he wouldn't tell me. Just said I was too young and had plenty of trouble already and to shut up before he kicked the puke out of me.

But how I wish I'd pushed it because I could sure use another way to forget the night Duda nailed the bank robbers. I can remember every minute of that night, every second, and I don't want to remember any of it.

It started just like another night of cruising. I'd finished setting pins just before eleven and went out the door, and Duda picked me up before I'd walked half a block and I got in the squad car. We rode around for a while and stopped at Johnny's, where Duda hit the game for some money. He must have done all right because he gave me five bucks for no reason, and then we went to Bonnie's and he went in and left me in the car to listen for the radio.

I was doing fine, looking at the shotgun bolted to the floor and dashboard in the car, thinking of Irene and just letting my mind float around the way you do. I think I might have dozed a little, or just dropped off, when the radio came to life.

"Duda?" It was Benny Martinez calling from the jail, the only other cop on duty at night, and he just stayed inside to listen for the phone. They never used police talk or numbers over the radio the way you see in movies, just names like they'd use on a telephone.

I took the microphone off the hanger on the dash and told Benny Duda wasn't in the car.

"Get him."

"Yeah, but not right way. He's in Bonnie's and you know what he'd do to me if I went in there."

"*Now!*" Benny's voice cut through like a butcher knife. "It's an emergency."

So I boiled out of the car. I mean Duda and I had talked about what we'd do if this came up and Duda had said if it's a real emergency I was supposed to bust in the house and get him. "Don't even knock," he'd said. "I just want to see the smoke around your behind from the afterburners."

118

I just hoped it was a real emergency because if it wasn't, if Benny was just fooling around, which he did sometimes, Duda would really let me have it.

I caught second going through Bonnie's back door, almost taking the screen off, and when I hit the back room, which turned out to be the kitchen, I cut loose with a bellow that almost peeled the paint off the walls.

"*Duda!*"

"Yo." It was muffled and came from a room on the left. I could just make out the doorway from the dim light off the clock on the kitchen stove. The lights were off.

"Benny called. It's an emergency."

"What about?" I heard bed springs creak and he came out of the door stark naked, carrying his clothes. "How long since he called?"

"Thirty seconds. Maybe a minute."

By this time he had his pants on. He handed me his harness and jacket and was pulling his shirt on as he made for the back door. "Let's *go*."

"Good luck, Nuts." Bonnie's voice sounded sleepy, like she might be talking with her head in a pillow and hair all over her face. Which made kind of a nice picture to think about while I followed Duda. Like in this movie I saw with Jane Russell where she's in love with a cowboy and one morning he comes in and finds her still in bed with her face buried in the pillow and that black hair spread all over. You could bet he didn't punch too many cows *that* morning.

"Duda here," was all he said when we got to the car. I was surprised to see he was almost completely dressed, just between the car and the house, while I'd been thinking of Jane Russell. "What is it, Benny?"

What it was, and some of it we didn't find out until later, was two bank robbers. A couple of days before they'd knocked over a bank down in Minneapolis, way south of Twin Forks, and then disappeared from sight. Everybody more or less figured they'd already made it to Canada or headed south for Mexico.

But instead they'd hidden for two days and then decided to head north. They probably would have made it except that they stopped in Erskine, a kind of truck-stop town twenty miles south of Twin Forks, for gas, and a waitress remembered their description from the radio. So she called the highway patrol and they didn't have a car close enough because some guy in a truck had hit a moose, and they called Benny.

The bank robbers' car went north when it left Erskine and the road north went straight through Twin Forks and on up to the Canadian border. If they drove hot it would only take them fifteen or so minutes to cover the distance, and I mean when we took out of that alley in back of Bonnie's, that old squad car flat *moved*.

Duda could drive. That's all there was to it. There's no way of checking, but we must have broken a ton of records getting out south of town. Twice he cut across peoples' lawns and ripped out fences. Gravel flew everywhere and the stink of burning rubber and hot engine was so strong it almost—not quite, but almost—cut through my fear that we'd crash or roll. I've never had a ride like that before in my life and probably never will again, if I can help it.

A mile south of town, and the speedometer was pegged once we broke city limits. Duda slammed on the brakes and screeched-slid the car so it was sitting sideways across the highway.

"Out!" He jerked the shotgun. "Grab your tail and cut for the timber. I don't want you around."

I couldn't believe my eyes. He was *smiling*.

So I made like I was heading back for town and when I'd gone about a hundred yards and Duda wasn't watching me anymore I cut down into the ditch and got in back of the brush row along the fence and worked back up until I was right across from where Duda and the car were waiting. He might beat me up later, but no way was I going to miss Duda and the bank robbers.

Which just goes to show you how dumb a guy can be. I mean afterward I wished I hadn't seen it. . . .

Waiting was the hard part. It was cold in the ditch, standing in the snow hunkered over so Duda couldn't see me in back of the brush, just wearing my leather jacket and no hat or gloves.

They didn't come and *didn't* come, and just about the time I was getting ready to say to heck with it and go back to the car and face the music for staying because I was certain they'd turned off—I even

121

stood up a little—right then I could see a change come over Duda.

He'd been leaning over the hood of the car looking down the highway south, smoking a cigarette, just holding the shotgun loose and easy, the barrel of the gun gray and stubby-looking and mean, aimed down the highway.

Suddenly he straightened and threw the cigarette away. I looked down the road but couldn't see or hear anything, so I turned back to Duda.

It was like a picture I saw once about a bullfighter—that's what happened to Duda. He knew they were coming—I don't know how, but he *knew* —maybe he smelled them the way animals do, and his whole body changed and his eyes changed and his mouth changed.

He stood tall and straight holding the shotgun and his back was arched and his gut was gone—I swear it—and his nostrils were open a little wider than usual and his mouth had this, well, peaceful smile on it like maybe he'd been worried about something and he wasn't worried anymore. He looked graceful, like that bullfighter—the shotgun kind of pointed out like an extra-long finger and his feet slightly apart and the whole curve of his body kind of flowing into the gun and south down the road.

I mean it was kind of beautiful.

Then I heard it. The whine of an engine coming way down the road, maybe two miles out across the cold flats, and I knew they were coming because nobody else would be driving that hard and I was afraid. They weren't going to stop for one cop and a car, they were going to go right over him and keep going and they were going to smash Duda into nothing and I realized right then that I loved Duda.

I loved him—not like Irene but different and more, and I didn't understand it except that he was all of me right then and they were going to kill him. He was like my father, only better, and then the car was there and what happened next is a blur.

Duda had the red light on top of the car going, so they knew he was a cop, and when they were about a quarter of a mile away they aimed off to one side to shoot around him on the shoulder.

And he waited. Like that bullfighter waiting for the bull coming down on him. He waited still and calm and peaceful, and when they were only a hundred yards away he fired just once and the double-ought buckshot out of that gun took the whole windshield out of the bank robbers' car.

The car screamed off the road into the ditch and for a couple of minutes there was nothing but sound as metal crashed and ripped and finally the car came to a stop in the ditch almost in front of where I was hiding.

And I thought, thank God it's over, and Duda is all right.

But it wasn't over.

The bank robbers were cut up some from the flying glass, but they weren't really hurt bad and they started to get out of the car with their hands up and I could see they were just a couple of young guys, hardly out of school, and one of them was crying and had snot running out of his nose. I was that close.

Duda waited until the first one cleared the car and then he raised the shotgun and I wanted to scream *no* but I couldn't make my throat work and Duda blew the top of his head off so the brains and bones just went everywhere.

The other one started screaming and crying and Duda just kind of flicked the barrel of the gun over a hair and ripped the whole chest out of him.

Like the rabbit I'd killed that first night they twitched and the one with no chest made kind of clawing motions at the snow and blood around him. I stared and then I looked up and Duda was watching them the way he'd watched that rabbit I'd killed, watching the life go out of them, and I started puking and running for town.

I ran all the way back, over a mile, trying to breathe and vomit while I was running. When I got there I didn't know what to do or where to go, so I got in the back of the Dodge and just sat there, curled up, for the rest of the night and most of the next day. And even though I was so tired the weariness came from my feet and went all up my body, I didn't sleep, didn't even doze, because how can you sleep when you love somebody like a father and he does that?

Chapter Fourteen

So I didn't see Duda for a while, the way you do when you want to drop back and look at something a little. I wasn't so mad as much as sick and I didn't know what to believe anymore because Duda had been just about everything there for a while and I'd really been looking up to him the way I would to a father, and everything he said was like law. Then he did that. . . .

So I just set pins and went to school and lived in the back of the Dodge.

Irene's folks found out about her condition and sent her away and I guess she didn't tell them it was Roger who did it because when I went over to see her one night her father met me at the door and half beat me to death with a shovel.

"Evil little scum!" he screamed at me. "You're nothing but trash." And he nailed me with the snow shovel next to the door. Cut the top of my head pretty bad, so I bled some, and I didn't stay around to argue with him.

Besides, I wasn't too sure he was wrong. I mean I wasn't thinking all that well and maybe I *was* evil, like Gib Nymen said, because even if I hadn't been the one to make Irene that way I was still around, and maybe that's all you have to do to be evil. Just be around when not-good things are happening, be part of them, like I was part of Duda and the bank robbers, even though I hadn't done anything. Because I didn't do anything to stop it, either.

And the following week I didn't say anything while the papers and people made a hero out of Duda and called him some kind of wonderful guy because he'd stopped two armed bank robbers singlehandedly. They gave him a medal and everything. And I didn't say a word to anyone.

Which makes me just about as evil as Roger for doing that to Irene, or Duda for blowing those two guys to pieces. . . .

I even went to the Reverend Peterson, who is a hypocrite because in public he says smoking is wrong and he smokes like a chimney himself in private, and asked him to tell me what makes somebody evil—I was thinking of it that much.

"My son," he said, which turned me off because I wasn't his son, "you're too young to be considering all the evil in the world."

That didn't do any good because I wasn't considering all the evil in the world, just a little of it in Twin Forks, and then only what I was personally involved in; I was having too much trouble with *that* to want to expand business. But I didn't expect much anyway, going to the church, so I wasn't disappointed. I've never had a lot of luck with churches. For the most part they just tell you what you already know and don't want to hear anyway.

So I just wandered from day to day like that, wondering how Irene was, setting pins, thinking about evil, and wondering if I was going nuts. Twice after I'd set pins Duda came by in the prowl car and stopped but I wouldn't get in and kept walking, so he drove on. Neither time did we say anything, but Duda had a kind of hard-hurt look around his eyes and I felt terrible because I wanted to get in the car and I was afraid to, afraid that I'd start asking dumb questions about why he killed those two guys when they had their hands up and wanted to surrender.

And then something happened that seemed really good at the time but turned out to be the second to the worst thing in my whole life.

Mom and Dad got off the sauce for almost a week. The minister came over one day and caught them both drunk and broke—broke for sure, because I'd been making runs on Mom's purse and there wasn't a dime in it. Right away they tried to make up to me, which they always did when they quit drinking, so I didn't expect much. They'd quit before for a day at a time, once for two days, and every time they'd make this big effort to fix things up with me, make up for all the beatings and screaming. I mean I'd been there, so I didn't pay much attention even when Mom cooked a big meal and Dad asked me if I wanted a new pair of hockey skates, which I didn't. I didn't even like to play hockey—which he didn't know, but it didn't matter. They weren't pounding on me or each other and they weren't screaming and breaking things, and that was enough.

But then they made three days without drinking and four, the longest they'd been sober since I could remember, and Dad came home from work that fourth day and said we were going up to visit Uncle Harvey the next day, on his farm up by Newfolden.

And we went, too, and they didn't drink or even talk about drinking, and we had an awfully good time. My cousin Harlen, who is the same age as me, took me over to the Ellisons' place, about a mile away, where these two girls lived, Kathy and Elaine Ellison, and they were our age and we had a rodeo to show off—the way you do.

I mean we didn't set out to have a rodeo, just to go over and see them because Elaine was pretty and Kathy wasn't ugly, either. But when we got there, Elaine started talking about this movie she'd seen at the drive-in that was all about a rodeo, and the next

128

thing you know Harlen is talking about riding wild steers, so we went out to the barn and eared down a big Holstein heifer because they didn't have any steers.

We flipped for the first ride and Harlen won and later I was glad. The back of the barn, outside, was nothing but a swamp of manure where the cows had been standing, and we were using the sliding back door on the barn—leading right into that swamp— for a chute for the ride. I didn't measure it, but I'll bet the gook out there was close to a foot deep and it smelled like the time I cleaned Gust's pigpen. I mean *rank*.

Well, we threw a rope around this heifer and she didn't even quiver, and Harlen climbed up on top of her and she *still* didn't mind, just chewed her cud and blinked.

Kathy and Elaine were all eyes while Harlen took the rope through his hand, and that's where the problem started. There was way too much rope for the standard bull riders' loop that just goes around the hand once, and Harlen didn't want a long tail of rope hanging around to get tangled up in, so he just kept wrapping it around his wrist and up his arm till it was all used up.

When he had rope wound halfway up to his elbow he looked at me, gave a tight little smile to Elaine and Kathy and said, "Outside!" Which is what rodeo cowboys say to the guy on the chute when they want the gates opened.

So I slid the doors open.

And the heifer stood there for a minute or so, looking out across the swamp of muck, and then she turned her big brown eyes up and looked at Harlen on her back, gave a kind of shrug, and stepped carefully out of the barn.

She must have been blowing herself out when we tightened the rope because when she gave that shrug it loosened up and Harlen slid down around her like water down a windowpane, until he was underneath her in the goop, and then he couldn't get loose because the rope was wrapped around his arm so many times.

I thought we were going to die, we laughed so hard—Elaine most of all. That heifer never kicked, never bucked, never once tried to hurt Harlen. All she did was walk around, back and forth, up and down, dragging Harlen through manure while he screamed words that even Duda probably didn't know and fought to get the rope off. I mean he had cow dung packed into his *ears,* and no part of him was clean.

And later on the way home with Mom and Dad I told them about it and we all laughed again and it was all right there for a while.

Too all right. Because I was all messed up what with Irene and Duda and the bank robbers and I'd had all these walls built up, so when Mom and Dad were whupping up on me or trying to stab me it wasn't like it was really my mom and dad working me over but two other drunk people. You either put those walls up or you go crazy trying to figure out why your mother would try to stab you with a butcher knife or your dad would try to choke you to death; you've got to make them into two other people, two strangers, and you don't listen to them or see them or even know they're related to you. They're like two dumb people you have to live with for some reason and not your mom and dad when you have the walls up.

But don't you just *know* that when they stayed off the juice for almost a week and we had those nice days there, like other people must have all the time, well, the first thing I did was start lowering the walls and looking at them like parents and I started to feel almost normal. I mean Dad and I talked about the old Dodge and he knew a lot about old cars, and I told them about setting pins and riding around with Duda but not the part about the bank robbers. And we all cried and said how it would be different now and it'd be better and they wouldn't drink, and it got pretty mushy. But nice. For a little there it was awfully nice and I wouldn't want to give the idea that it was all bad. It wasn't—parts of that time were so nice they almost made the bad go away by comparsion.

But when they'd been dry a week it all went to pieces.

I came home from setting pins and fighting Kenny Sova and I was really wrung out. I'd set double alleys because Reggie was sick and Kenny had kicked me

131

in the gut and I was still half sick when I got home and walked into the house and they were both drunk, wild drunk, as Duda would have said, and fighting and screaming, and they didn't even see me sneak back to my room. I thought of going out to the Dodge, but it was too cold and I was shot. So I got into my room and took off my clothes and lay back on my bed and cried and tried to find the walls to put them back up, but it was just too much, all of it, and I fell asleep crying and without the walls.

I don't know how long I slept, but when I woke up it was still dark and Mom was sitting on the side of my bed and she was drunk and crying and moaning about how terrible she was and Dad, too.

And I didn't really wake up but went back to half-sleep and half dreamed—or I *think* I dreamed—about Irene. She was in bed with me, and then it all got mixed up, the dream and Irene and Duda and Mom. It all tumbled and tumbled through my mind because there were no walls to stop it and I wasn't asleep and I wasn't awake and I wasn't doing what I was doing but I *was* all of those things, too, asleep and awake and doing it. . . .

The next thing I was outside, walking in my shorts, heading for the railroad yards. I didn't want to live anymore or *be* anymore, and the picture of Irene's father beating me with a shovel and screaming "Evil!" was in my mind and the memory of Gib Nymen whipping me with the trace chain.

And then I was climbing the coal tower in the

railroad yards. Sometimes Reggie and I would go up there at night and catch pigeons because they roosted there and it was the only high place I knew where the fall might kill you and fix it so you wouldn't need those walls.

And I think I must have sat there for a time, up in the tower, listening to the pigeons cooing because it's such a peaceful sound and my mind right then was an explosion and I needed something peaceful. I was just getting ready to fall out the opening in the bottom where the coal used to go when they still used steam locomotives, I was just kind of slipping over when Duda grabbed me.

I fought him and tried to break away, but he was too strong and I screamed. I remember screaming and I must have somehow screamed what I'd dreamed because he wrapped me up in his jacket and carried me back down the ladder and he was crying and saying, "Don't worry, kid, I love you and Bonnie loves you and Carl loves you and it's going to be all right. . . ."

And it was the music again, the music he used that night with Carl and Gust used with the bull, where you don't hear the words by themselves but all strung together in a song, and it was like salve on a burn and I just hung there in his arms.

Duda took me to Bonnie's but I don't remember the ride. All I can remember is being on Bonnie's bed, with Bonnie sitting on one side wiping my forehead with a damp cloth and Duda sitting on the

133

other side, and these huge tears were cutting down his cheeks and his lips were all wrinkled down and he was saying,

"Ahh, Bonnie, why are we so rotten? Why are people such miserable garbage?"

And I could have answered except that Bonnie handed me something warm in a glass and made me drink it and I went out like I'd been hit with an ax handle. When the dark cloud came down I was trying to tell Duda about the walls, how it was when you lowered the walls that people became miserable garbage, but I never got it out. . . .

Which is really sad because if Duda had known about the walls, hadn't lowered them, he might still be alive.

Chapter Fifteen

"How is it that something good can come from something bad?" I asked Duda once while we were driving around. It was after the night in the coal tower and things were going pretty well. "I mean that whole mess with Mom and booze and all was so awful. . . ."

"Don't think about it," Duda cut in. "Until it's covered with dust and the dust is layered with dirt, don't drag that one out and think about it. It happens, that's all."

"I wasn't. I just meant how can what's happening now, which is good, come from something so bad?"

"Life is like a rubber ball." He paused to scratch his belly. "You throw it down and it bounces back up. *I* don't know how it happens. You being a wise guy?"

"No. I'll never be a wise guy again."

"Yeah." He reached over and tapped me on the shoulder. "I know. Just talking, you know how it goes. . . ."

But it *was* good, right then, and it all came from something bad, and I still haven't figured out how that can happen but I'd like to because if it ever happens again I want to understand it.

The next morning after that night I woke up and Duda and Bonnie were still sitting there, and they were holding hands and sort of smiling, and when Duda saw my eyes were open he looked down and smiled. A real smile. Not the hard one.

"How is it?" he asked.

But I couldn't talk about anything right then, so I nodded, not that it was all right, just that I was still alive and knew he was there and Bonnie was there.

"Don't talk, just listen." Duda pointed his chin at Bonnie. "We spent the night jawing over you and came up with some ideas. How would you like to have a different set of parents?"

I looked over at Bonnie and she nodded.

"Yeah," Duda cut in. "Me and Bonnie. My marriage isn't working so hot, and it turns out me and Bonnie are in love, isn't that something?"

I started to say I thought it was just great, but Duda waved me down.

"So I'm going to get a divorce and me and Bonnie are going to get married and we're going to adopt you, runt. How's that?"

But I couldn't answer him because I was bawling like a baby and Bonnie leaned down and kissed me on the forehead and Duda ruffled my hair. It *was* all right, it was so good nothing in my life will *ever* be that good again—that's how it was, and I reached out and put my hand on top of theirs and after a long time went back to sleep and there weren't any dreams.

And all of that came from something bad, evil. And I would like to stop the story of Duda here and tell how he got his divorce and married Bonnie and they adopted me and we bought a farm and I got a new engine for my Dodge and Duda showed me how to drive the way he drives and there was nothing but good from that evil for the rest of our lives.

That's how it would end in a movie, with Rock Hudson playing Duda and Doris Day playing Bonnie, and that's how it *should* end, and that's how I dream of it ending almost every night, until I wake up sweating and remember that it isn't a movie and it doesn't end that way. And then I sit and try to think of what good will come when the ball bounces back up again.

Because I wasn't the only one who lowered his walls and got nailed, got caught by evil.

Duda changed, too. He lowered *his* walls when

he decided to fall in love with Bonnie and to adopt me. He lost the hard edges, the toughness that he used to keep things away from him, and maybe those hard edges weren't good and maybe they weren't what Duda really wanted to be. But they're what he used, they're what got him through the night.

They're what kept him alive, those edges, and because of me he lost them or dropped them . . . me and Bonnie, but I've never said that to her because it would just upset her more than she needs to be upset. Like me.

What happened was that he lowered the walls just at the wrong time, just when he needed them most, and in that he wasn't so much different from anybody else, I suppose, but it isn't very nice to be the reason for it all. . . .

I'd set pins all night, or until eleven, and I'd pretty much moved into Bonnie's except that I'd ride with Duda until he got off and then we'd both go to Bonnie's.

Anyway, four in the morning rolled around and Duda was just heading in to change shift when Benny called.

"Duda?"

"Yo," he worked the microphone with a flourish, "what do you need?"

"Got a runaway kid." We could hear Benny shuffling papers. "Name of Walgren. Richard Walgren."

"Trinity minister's kid?" Duda smiled. "Isn't that the one?"

"Right." Benny ruffled some more papers and it made a staticky sound on the radio. "He's fifteen.

Took his old man's car and headed out west of town in the direction of Warren to see his girl friend."

Duda laughed and I smiled. "So what's the big hassle?"

"Hey, *I* don't know." We could hear Benny snort in the mike. "The old man called and wants us to get him back—said the kid was disturbed. You want to mess with it, or should we just leave it for the day people?"

Duda gave me a wink. "Probably just in love. We'll run out west for a while and see if he's along the road—it's been icy and he might have cracked up. If we don't see him in ten miles or so, I'll come back in and hang it up."

"Right." Benny signed off and Duda hung up the car mike.

Warren is a town smaller than Twin Forks, about eighteen miles straight west. Down the road about eight miles out of Twin Forks there is a big S-curve with really wide ditches, shallow and curved up at the edges into lips.

We found Richard in the ditch at the S-curve. He'd tried to take it too fast and there was some ice and it was cold, awfully cold for early spring, and he'd gone into that shallow ditch so his car was sitting sideways to the road.

"Know anything about the kid that might help me?" Duda asked as we drove up.

I shook my head. "Seen him around school, you know, but I don't know him. He's a minister's kid and I'm, well, I don't know what I am."

"Yeah."

Duda stopped the squad car on the road sort of angled over, so the headlights were down on Richard's car in the ditch. Richard was standing on the other side of his car, so all you could see were his shoulders and head. I could see he had a flattop and that it wouldn't stay up just like mine, and that he was having trouble with pimples and his eyes were wide and he was scared, scared deep.

Duda sat in the car for a second or two and looked at the car and Richard down in the ditch with a small sneer on his lips, the old Duda, and then he got out and stood next to the prowl car and his body arched and his gut disappeared like the bullfighter, like he did the night of the bank robbers, and I thought man, he's doing it again, turning into whatever it is he was on that night, and I got a tight feeling in my stomach.

But then he shrugged, looked over to me, let his gut out a little and relaxed and walked to the front of the prowl car, so he was standing between the headlights with one ear cocked over into the fur collar on his jacket to keep it warm and his hands in his pockets.

"Hey, puke kid," he yelled down at Richard, "don't you know how to drive?"

From that point on everything seemed to move in slow motion and all at once because not only had Richard stolen his dad's car but he'd broken into the gun case and taken a deer rifle as well, only the minister hadn't said anything about it and I hope his guts burn in hell forever for not saying anything.

I saw Richard raise the barrel of the rifle over the

140

top of his car, like he was pulling it through syrup, and I reached for the door handle and screamed "NOOOOOO!" while I was opening the door because Duda had put the walls down and wasn't ready, wasn't ready, wasn't ready.

Then fire roared from the end of the rifle barrel and Richard's shoulder bounced with the recoil and Duda slammed back into the front of the squad car and blood came out his back and covered the windshield and I was out, out of the car and moving to the front while Duda started to go down.

He didn't fall, he just sat slowly, sliding down the front of the car until he was sitting and on the way down his hand brought his gun out of his harness and it fired once, then twice, and Richard went down and I was next to Duda.

He was staring at his feet, just staring like that— all blank—like he couldn't see that far, and the whole front of him was blood and torn open and I got down beside him and he looked sort of at me but not really, like through me, and he said,

"No."

And the life went out of him, out of his eyes, out of his body, out of him, out and out and out, and I grabbed him and tried to hold it in but it wouldn't stay even though I begged, and the little jerks of steam from his nostrils stopped. Just stopped. And he messed. And he died—like the rabbit, like the bank robbers, with his hands making little clawing motions at the road he died, and I wanted to die with him but couldn't.

I guess I called Benny on the radio but I don't

remember it, because he came out and got me and took me back to town and dropped me at Bonnie's place and I walked into her kitchen and she already knew because Benny had told her.

"Oh, Bonnie," I said. "He's dead. Duda's dead."

And I sank to the kitchen floor and couldn't stop crying and crying and crying and she got a quilt from someplace and brought it into the kitchen and sat down next to me and wrapped the quilt around both of us and we sat there holding each other and crying all day, never talking, just crying until there wasn't anything left and then we just sat and that's the story of Duda.